Thimble

A ROMANCE AND A LOVE STORY OF THE YOUNG AND OLD

ROBERT CORY PHILLIPS

Order this book online at www.trafford.com
or email orders@trafford.com

Most Trafford titles are also available at major online book retailers.

Printed in the United States of America.

ISBN: 978-1-4907-4515-2 (sc)
ISBN: 978-1-4907-4517-6 (hc)
ISBN: 978-1-4907-4516-9 (e)

Library of Congress Control Number: 2014915088

Trafford rev. 08/21/2014

 www.trafford.com
North America & international
toll-free: 1 888 232 4444 (USA & Canada)
fax: 812 355 4082

Contents

Acknowledgements

I wish to thank a great man. A man that served his country. A man that I will always think of. A man that told me this story. This man was my Uncle Ernest. Today, I look back and try to remember the story that had a meaning to me then and now. I was nine years old sitting on a pile of wood that he had cut for the fireplace. I remember watching his eyes as he told me about the planes in the air. I watched him have tears in his eyes as he told me about the love that two people had for each other. A story that had a happy ending. A story that I will never forget…A story of the young and old….

Funny thing is, a tiny silver thimble made it all happen and a love that will never die. For two people it will live

Forever….

I would also like to thank my publisher and the staff of creative people and for their time, help, and believing in this novel.

Thank you, and hope your Romance and Love will be forever.

And to Mrs. Sherry Jolly of Executive Aid Secretarial Service for her excellent editing, proofreading, and suggestions. Thank you.

Epigraph

Love lasts forever. There are many different types of loves in our lives. We love our mother, father, first love, and many in-between loves. The one that we remember is the love that lasts and lasts forever. The grave will take us away from the world, but the love we have for each other will last forever. That will never die. The colors of love and romance are many. Even the stains are beautiful.

The first love we ever had will carry us into the world as a bright light. The last love we have as we lie on the bed of death will be the best of all.

Robert Cory Phillips

Author Biography

Robert Cory Phillips was born in Nashville, Tennessee He went in service in the Marine Corp and served his country. Later years, he went to Hollywood, California where he did films as an actor but found his love behind the camera as a photographer. There he began to write. The stories that came from notes over the years have now been written down, and several books have been published. This novel is a romance novel of the young and old. "Thimble" has given him a look that he has wanted.

The colors of life.

Now living back in his home state of Tennessee, he now finds happiness in his writing. This shows in his work and makes the reader keep turning the pages of his books.

Robert is truly the master of great reading material. From children's books, to great fiction, to romance, he has created a following of his work both with the young and old as well.

Thimble will always be remembered as one of the best of his works.

An American boy and a French girl will stay on your mind, always.

"Thimble"

**This is a true story, of love, two people,
And a small tiny, Thimble.**

They stood in the doorway. As their lips parted, their eyes met. A nervous smile and a touch on his cheek, her hands smoothed the collar of his uniform. She touched the star on his chest and closed her eyes as his hand ran through her long brown hair.

Bombs fell in the distance. "I must go."

Her fingers traced his lips. "I know."

His strong arms wrapped around her for the last time as he kissed a falling tear from her blue eyes. "But, I will be back."

The smell of his uniform told her that he cared. "I know you will."

The roar of the planes flew over the building. He tilted her chin up to him. "You're my girl."

She kissed his hand with a faint smile. "Yes, I am, forever."

His hands held her face. "I'll be back." He stepped back looking at her. "I'll be back, I love you." He turned and took a step.

"No, wait."

He turned to see her go to a small sewing basket.

She picked up the basket and a smile came as she took a silk scarf and a cap from the basket.

"I finished it last night. A scarf for your neck and a cap for your hair."

She put the long silk scarf around his neck. He took his uniform hat off as she put the cap on his head. She smiled. "Now, you are perfect."

He kissed her hands as she adjusted the cap.

"I feel perfect."

She took his hand and placed a small silver thimble in it.

He held his finger up looking at the thimble. "What is this?"

"It's for luck, so you want get hurt."

He wiggled his finger with a chuckle and a smile.

"I wore it when I was knitting your cap and scarf."

He kissed it and put it in his jacket pocket. "I'll bring it back to you." He picked up his bag and walked down the steps. He stopped and blew her a kiss. "Love you."

With that, he ran down the street with the scarf trailing behind him. She leaned against the door as tears ran down her face.

"Love you."

Planes dropped their bombs for hours and hours.

It was war. The building and the doorway were soon gone. Smoke, fire, and fog filled the air.

Years later...The world after...The War...

An old woman, wrinkled face, dirty dress and torn, tattered shawl stood in an alley. A man came out of a building and dumped trash and scraps of food in the large bin. A loud sound came from the bin as it closed.

The man looked around and went back into the building. Slowly, the old woman took a few steps as she pushed her cart.

She walked through the fog and musty smell of the night. She looked down the alley and adjusted the black patch from her right eye. She wiped the moisture with the long scar as her shaking dirty hands searched the bin for food or maybe a drink left in a bottle of wine.

The street lamp was dim, with the fog drifting in the night. There she sat. Picking bread in small bits. She rocked back and forth like a baby of two. A tear ran down from her bad eye and across the scar. She sat mumbling as she ate the bread.

A tapping noise made her stop rocking as she cocked her head listening to the tap, tap, tap, getting closer to her. Quickly she hides the bread. With her head down, she looked into the fog and could see a cane tapping and a foot dragging another foot.

With her head bowed down she held out both hands together. The tapping stopped. For a moment the air was still and the tapping slowly started again.

"A penny, a nickel."

An old man stood looking down at her. He dragged his right foot close to his side and leaned on the cane.

"A penny, a nickel." She said again.

The old man looked up into the fog and the dim light.

"It's cool tonight." He looked at her shaking hands. "I ain't got much." His left hand touched his empty sleeve of his coat. "I say, it's cool tonight."

The old woman nodded her head. "Yes, yes it is."

He put the cane between his legs and with his left hand fished in his coat pocket. He pulled his hand out and looked at his change.

"Don't have much. Sixteen, seventeen cents, all I got."

The old woman shook her head. "Don't want it all."

He chuckled. "Thought I had nineteen cents." Again, he fished in his pocket. "Nope, guess not, just this old bent thimble. Had it for years. Don't have a foot or an arm, but,".... He laughed, "I got this old bent thimble. Its good luck you know."

He put the change and the thimble in her hands. "Maybe it will bring you good luck." A, ha, came from him. "It did me."

The old woman's one good eye searched her hands.

The tap, tap, tap, of the cane slowly disappeared into the fog of the night.

She dropped the change and held the sliver thimble to the light.

Bombs, fire, smoke, exploded in her mind. She kissed the thimble as thoughts of a young man who ran down the street with a scarf and cap. She started to cry as she looked into the heavy night's fog. She again looked at the tiny thimble.

"David, David …. Was that you?"

"Thimble" Starts Now...

Eight-year-old Cory sat on a pile of cut firewood glazing out to the hills of bear trees and a gray sky. It was a cool winter's day. The sound of his uncle's ax chopping logs. Ernest stopped and looked at Cory. He put his ax down and sat beside Cory. "What you thinking about boy?"

Cory put his hands in his jacket still looking out at the sky.

"Uncle Ernest, what is love about?"

His uncle laughed out loud. "Well son that is a hard question to answer. There are many kinds of love. Some people love their cars, their house, and their money and of course they love each other. You love your dog don't you? You see there are all kinds of love."

Cory looked at him. "You ever been in love?"

Ernest stood putting his hand in his pocket. He took a few steps and turned to Cory. "Yep."

"What kind of love were you in Uncle Ernest?"

Ernest sat down again looking out at the sky and thinking about his first love. "It was people love. It was my wife. We were sweethearts from the first day we met."

Cory moved close to his uncle. They both sat quite for a while.

"Did you ever love something or a thing?"

"No, but I know people that have. Let me tell you a story about that very thing. When I was in the service a long time ago, I met an amazing fellow. His name was David Hunt. We met in a hospital overseas. Never will forget the story he told me. It was in Paris, France he told me that they met. Her name was Denise I believe, been so long I forget now, but the best I remember it was. Anyway this is the way the story goes."

PART 1

PART 1

Chapter 1

As a boy of eight years there are things
I want to know, … Like,
Why is the earth round?
Why is brown, brown?
Why is the sky blue?
Why are there me and you?
Why do trees reach for above?
Why do people fall in love?

It All Started Here... Paris France...

Denise Val Jean was only fifteen when her mother and father were killed in an automobile accident. It was on a snow skiing trip in the high mountains at night when the car skidded off the road. All the church people gathered around Denise to give her comfort. As an only child it was hard for her to understand that she was alone.

For a long while families from the church brought food and helped with the up keep of the large house. Tears would fall at night as she would look at pictures of good times with her mother and father.

As time passed, tears were replaced with her winning smile and good looks. Her short brown hair grew to her waist. Her candy blue eyes became an ocean blue.

Her French accent became clear and sexy. Confidence grew with her tall body. Her tears vanished and so did many of the church people. School was easy for her. Reading had given her a way to enjoy time to herself. Romance and love stories told her that she was not alone. At school she was a perfect student. With the highest of grades, her teachers admired her for the way she had raised herself after her parents had died. She would walk home alone with books in hand and always wave at the neighbors along the way. A night of reading poems was her way of escaping loneliness.

She would write in her book of poems words that meant things to her only. Her mother had given her this talent. It was told that she would see a bird flying in the sky and she would write about it. Or children playing in the park. She was a very romantic person and loved words.

Then one day, David Hunt came into her life. Sitting only a few seats away from her at school they would exchange glances and small smiles. From smiles to small talk, to a soda at the café, to long walks, to a kiss. She was never alone again.

She stood looking out of the large open window down the dusty road when her bright eyes began to smile and her heart began to beat faster. A way in the distance was David on his bicycle heading her way.

She watched as the tall good-looking boy paddled his way to the big house. David was not like other boys she knew. He was different and knew what he wanted in life.

He was an American. She thought his accent was funny. The time they spent together was like a storybook romance with no end. She watched as he pushed the bike the last few steps to the gate.

David parked his bicycle by the white wooden fence and adjusted his blue tie. He spat in his hand and patted down his hair. His eyes searched the many windows of the large house. Shadows of the house fell to the left side as the soft warm wind blew.

He picked a bunch of cut flowers from the bikes basket, smiled and put them behind him. It had been love at first sight. She was beautiful and amazing. Sitting three seats away, their glances at each other told the story. The teacher looked at her watch then at the clock on the wall.

"Okay everybody class is over."

As the kids gathered their things and were leaving, Mrs. Meadows called out. "David you and Denise stay."

David looked at Denise. She sneaked a peek at David and sat back down.

The room was quite except for the tapping of Mrs. Meadow's pencil. "OK you two, these notes you pass have got to stop. I don't know if they are love notes or answers to questions, but they end here today. Got me?"

She pointed to David. David shyly nodded. "Yes ma'am."

"Good… now Denise I expect more from you. You set an example for the other girls. No more notes."

Denise nodded. "Yes ma'am." Mrs. Meadow's crooked smile appeared. "I was young too you know."

Later that day….

David stood at the front door and knocked. Denise shook her white dress and slowly opened the door. "Hi, can Denise come out and play?"

She looked behind her and then to David.

"She is not here right now, can I help you?"

"Well I'll come back later. Oh, here, these are for her."

Denise's eyes lit up. "For me? I mean for her."

David smiled. "Yes, for you silly." They laughed and went in the house.

David sat watching her arrange the flowers in a vase. Her fingers gently touched each flower. "They are so soft and pretty. Thank you, merci."

David touched her hand as their eyes met.

"A flower so soft, a touch of your hand, a smile in your eyes, a grain of sand. Small things I ask for to grow in your heart, for today and always may we never part." She kissed his hand. "That was beautiful." The kiss was one, only one that they could share. Denise laughed.

"If only Mrs. Meadows could see us now. Love notes or questions. They are love notes and I save them all."

"You did? Boy bet you have a big box because there are a lot more to come."

Time stood still as they gazed into each other's eyes and soul.

"Let's take a walk down by the stream." The warm summer winds changed to a cool breeze as they lay in the tall grass by the stream. The pale blue sky reached across the hills in the far distance as silver white clouds passed in the wind. David reached for her hand. "Tell me about yourself, about your father and mother. I want to know all about you."

Denise rolled over with a small yellow flower in her hand and held it to the sky. "Okay, what do you wish to know?"

"Everything." "Well my father was an architect. He designed tall buildings. I use to watch him at night as he worked drawing blue prints and he would make a model of the building he was working on. I loved him very much. My mother was a teacher. She taught English for kids in the seventh grade. She had a wonderful way with words and she taught me many things that even today I use when I write. She was a soft woman with a pleasant smile that made people like her right away. As for me, I love to write poems. I wrote one for you and maybe someday I will read it to you. I love to tickle words."

"Tickle words? What do you mean?"

"Okay, there are many ways to say things. Like, I love you. You can say, my heart breathes your breath. Or, loving you is my life," she whispered in his ear.

"As for what we just did. I never knew making love could feel this way. You make me feel so special. You make me to ask for more. More of you, more of your kisses. I don't want it to ever end." Denise waited to see if David was happy with what she had said. "Okay Mr. David Hunt it's your turn to tell me about yourself." "Well let's see. As a young boy, I was a boy scout. I even helped an older lady across the street. I got a badge for that to. School was pretty easy for me. I liked lunch time best of all." Denise laughed. "Go on." David thought about his friends back home. "In school I had a very good friend. His name was Jessie. We had a lot of good times and a few bad times." He went on.

"Guess I might as well tell you about the bad time we had. One day he told me about a home coming party for the football team and that we should go. He asked if I could get my father's car. I told him I would ask for it and I did. My father told me the rules and I agreed. So, that night we went to the lake to see what was going on. There was a lot of people there and lots of girls. There was loud music, food, and beer.

It wasn't long till Jessie brought two girls for me to meet. I forget their names right now but they were ready to do most anything.

Jessie handed me a beer and I told him no that my father had said no drinking. So anyway, it was getting late and I told Jessie that we should be getting home. He asks if we could take the girls home. I said sure. Well this is the bad part. I guess I was distracted from my driving by the girl sitting next to me and the noise coming from the back seat. As I was driving alone, pretty fast, out of know where a police car came up behind me with the red lights flashing. So I pulled over and stopped. I watched as he came up to the car. He asked for my driver's permit as he saw I was under age. He looked in the back and saw Jessie and the girl and saw a beer can on the floor. He told all of us to get out of the car and show I.D.s. We all were under age and beer in the car. Well guess what. We all went to jail.

We had to call our parents to come get us out. Dad was not very happy about this. We were released and a court date was set for us to appear. I never will forget that day. The judge called me into his chamber. Talking about fear, well I was. He said to me, "David Hunt, I know your father. He is a good man and I know he taught you better that to let you drink and drive." I told him that I did not have anything to drink that night. My legs shook as he told me to stand up so did my hold body. "David, I am going to go easy on you this time. No jail time but I am taking your driver's permit away for two years. And if you do drive, you go to jail." I assured him that I would not drive and there would never be beer in any car that I drove ever again.

That night at home was worst that the judge's office.

My father and mother sat looking at me in a way I will never forget. They didn't have to say a word. All I remember was that I kept saying, "I'm sorry." David looked at Denise. "Well that is my bad side. Can we change the subject?" Denise leaned over and kissed him on his cheek. "Thank you for telling me your story. What happen to your friend Jessie and the girls?"

"Well as for Jessie, he was grounded for several months. His father was transferred on his job to another city and we lost touch. The girls, I don't know about them."

David sat up looking at the stream running over the rocks.

"Would you read me some of your poems?"

"Someday I will, I promise but for now you tell me a poem."

He sat thinking then turned to her and held her hand.

"Time that is what it's all about. The endless stream of water. A passion that will never end. A love that starts and last till the last breath. You are my last breath."

Denise knelt with her arms around him. "I love you and you are my last breath."

David looked at her searching for answers. "But what if God should part us?"

She smiled and touched his nose. "Your name would be my last breath."

His mind drifted off with her answer. "Come on, it's getting late and cold."

The rest of the day was spent studying and gazing at each other. Denise held his hand. "What are you going to do tomorrow?"

"Tomorrow I have to work at Mr. Fisher's store."

"Do you like it there?"

"It is the money that I like and Mr. Fisher is a good man." She giggled.

"I have known him all my life. I like him to."

"Can I ask you for something?"

"I will try to answer you if I can, what you ask?"

"Can I have another kiss?" Again she giggled as a little girl.

"Only if I can kiss you back."

Chapter 2

When I grow up I want to work,
With smart people,
That isn't a jerk,
With people that teach me
What I need to know,
That will help me grow,
One day at a time…

The Store....

A small bell tinkled as Mr. Fisher walked in his store.

"Morning David."

"No sir, it's a good morning."

"Oh you young people know everything. What you got there?"

"Just a book I write in sometimes."

Mr. Fisher chuckled. "A love story I bet it is."

David tucked it in his shirt. "Looks like rain, think it will?"

"Hope not, we need rain but we need customers to." With that he went into the back of the store. David followed quickly.

"Mr. Fisher, I need to talk to you."

"Sure son anytime."

"I'm eighteen and thinking that I might have to go you know, to war."

Mr. Fisher put a small box on the shelf. "You know son, you might and again you might not. I think the war is a long way off from here. I wouldn't worry if I were you."

"But what if it were true? There are things that I want to do. I want to get married someday, have a family, a dog."

"Well tell you what. Follow your heart. Don't believe all you hear. Do what I do, live every day one day at a time."

"Guess you are right, one day at a time."

Breaking News

"So, what do you want to do now?"

Denise lay in his lap thinking. "Well, we have the house all by our self."

"Denise, there is something on my mind. What if I had to go away? Say to war."

"War? That is the craziest thing ever. There is not a war."

"Yes it is and it is getting close to us. I heard people talking. They say it may come here."

Denise sat up. "Look at me. You are not going anywhere you got that you silly American."

"I know, but what if?"

"If, is not a word. David, we have plans don't we? You want to fly a plane?"

"But…"

"No buts about it. Why would you want to leave me?"

David stood and went to the window looking out at the sky. "I would never leave you. Yes, there are things I want to do and you are a part of everything I want to do. Would you stop me from going if I had to go to war?"

She went to him and hugged him. "You must do what you must do."

Sounds came from the radio.

"We have breaking news. The talks of the war are getting the attention of the government. If peace talks do not bring results, there is a chance of the worse."

He looked at Denise. "See."

Denise sat listening to the radio. Suddenly she turned to David. "Have you talked to your father about this?" David went to the radio and turned it off. Her eyes followed him. The room was still.

David stood by the window looking out at the sky. "No, he is very busy at the Embassy and that is a very busy office. But you know, maybe I should. He would know what is going on."

"Yes, the French Embassy is a busy place, but I am sure that he would find time for his son. Why don't you talk to him when he gets home tonight?"

"Ha, you might not believe this but I haven't seen him for a week now. Mother says that he is working on a very special project. Maybe it is the war."

"David the war is a long way off. It will not affect us here in Paris. Look at the sky. Do you see anything up there but the birds? Do you hear anything except the wind and the sound of my heart?"

Denise hugged him. Their eyes met. The feeling they had for each other was love and of caring. The kiss was long, and strong feelings made all the thoughts of the war go away. Denise whispered in his ear.

"I love you. Would you like to go down by the stream and lay in the tall grass?" A simple smile came to her. "It is a beautiful day to make love."

It was. Denise breathed deeply as David penetrated her. His strong body held her down. He stroked her long dark hair. Their kiss again was long and loving as their bodies melted together.

The warm wind blew the tall grass as the clear blue sky above and a white cloud floated by.

"I love you so much. I wished this would never end. I do not want you to ever leave me." David hovered above her. "I will always have you in my heart. My love for you will always be."

Denise walked down by the stream of running water. She filled her hands with the water and watched it slide through her fingers. "David, America is a strong country right? Do you have wars there?"

David went to her. "In America, no, but we help other countries when they need help."

She gathered more water in her hands. "Will America help France?"

"Yes of course."

"Then France is safe right."

"Very safe and don't believe everything you hear on the radio."

"Oh David you have a way to make me feel very secure. Merci and thank you very much."

It was as it should have been. David lay in his bed that night thinking about the war, their lovemaking and what was to come. It seemed as everything was the same, but everything was different. He only knew one thing and that was Denise was right for him. He also knew that his father had all the answers to the war if there was any war to be in Paris of anywhere in the world. He rolled over looking at the picture of Denise on his night stand. With a smile he closed his eyes and soon slumber came to him.

Chapter 3

My dad is wise and smart as can be,
One day we sat under a tree,
"Son, if I can help you show you the way,
Just let me know, I'm here to stay,
If I can answer a question for you,
I hope my answers will guide you
Always"

Talking Hurts

"It's ready." The call for dinner went through the house. David sat staring at the silent radio. Mrs. Hunt came in to the living room. "Did you hear me? It's ready." She stood looking at her son's blank stare. Slowly she sat by his side.

"David, is something wrong? You look as if is the end of the world. Did you and Denise have a fight? … David, I'm talking to you."

He took her hand looking for answers. "Mother, I need to know about the war that I hear about. Is it real? Is Paris in trouble? Will we be going back to America?"

She dropped her head and rubbed his hands.

"Son, I don't know. There is a war. It is real, but as far as Paris, we will have to trust in God. I would suggest that you talk to your father. He would know more about things like the war. He will be home tonight later if you are concerned about leaving or staying here in Paris."

It was a quiet dinner as David and his mother sat eating. Only the sound of a fork on the plate was heard. David tapped on the table.

"When will he be home?"

Mrs. Hunt stood and gathered the plates. "Soon, would you like anything else? We have ice cream, Strawberry is your favorite."

"No thanks. I will be in my room. Would you tell dad I want to talk to him, no matter what time it is when he gets home, okay?"

"David, I don't want you to get upset no matter what he says about the war. We are safe and have friends to help in any case. Now, you go on and don't worry about a thing."

He stood by the door. "No matter what time it is, tell him for me."

David lay in his bed looking at the ceiling and thinking about Denise. She was all the things that he wanted. They had plans to go back to America.

A life that he could show her that she had only dreamed of. He thought of the two years he had been in Paris and the great times they had had.

Sleep came to him as he drifted into it with dreams of another life.

"Father Son Talk"

Hours had passed. A light tapping on the door came. Mr. Hunt slowly opened the door and stepped in. He put his briefcase down and went to the bed. He stood at the bedside looking at his son sleeping. His thoughts were of the time that he wished that he could spend with his son. The times that he had wished that he could have spent fishing, playing ball, laughing, or just together with him.

Slowly he sat on the bed. He reached for David's hand. "David, son," Slowly David stirred and opened his eyes. A big smile came to him. He sat up and put his arms around his father.

"Dad, you made it. Wow it's good to see you. I have really missed you. How have you been?" A big hug and a kiss on the cheek was what David had needed.

"I am just fine son. The only thing I can say is I'm sorry son for all the times I have not given you. You and your mother are the world to me. I just wish I could spend more time with both of you, but my work…"

"I know dad. If it wasn't for you, the world would just fall apart." They laughed at this. The mood changed.

David sat holding his father's hand.

"Dad, I know you are an important man at the Embassy. You know everything that is going on, I mean about the war. Dad, is Paris in danger? I keep hearing about the Germans and about how they may want to go to war. Is that true?"

Mr. Hunt stood and walked to the window. He turned to David and shook his head.

"We don't know for sure. They have no reason to, but it is very real that they might. There is a problem everywhere. My Embassy says that it is very possible and soon, but we can't say for sure. This is a very diplomatic place we are in. I can tell you for sure one thing, we, your mother and you are very safe."

"It's not about being safe dad, what about Paris? What can I do? I want to help France and Paris."

His father looked at him.

"I am an American in this country." Mr. Hunt again looked out the window. The stars were bright in the sky. He turned to David.

"Come look at the night. See the sky? See all the stars? David, you always said you wanted to fly a plane." Mr. Hunt walked to him and sat down. "Well this might be something you could do for both countries."

David looked puzzled. "What do you mean dad?"

"Well son, you could join the French Air Force as an American pilot. Fly food, troops, supplies, all kinds of help. You already know about flying a plane. Now may be your chance to do what you always wanted to do."

David's mind raced with the idea... A way to help.

"Wow dad, I never thought of that. If there was a war, I could be a part of it."

"But son, there is a danger involved. Maybe I could help you stay where it is safe. I don't want you too close to what might happen if there were a war."

David thought as he walked around the room. "Ok dad, how do I start?"

"Well you start with joining the French Air Force, Officer's school, training, and you are off. Maybe I can pull a few strings. But son, you need to give it a lot of thought and then there is Denise."

Weeks went by...

David walked all around town thinking about the war, Denise, school, and what he should do. On one hand there was the will to help and serve France. One the other hand he was an American and this was not his fight. Days and dark nights went by.

The thought of flying a plane was in his mind. Flying a plane for another country. If anything, he should fly for his country. Then there was Denise.

His love for her was the kind of love that had grown for the past two years. They had been together almost every day.

They had schooled for two years together.

They had loved and made love. How would she take it if she knew that he was thinking about going to war for France? What would she say about him leaving her?

How should I tell her? Life was so simple before all this. Fighting in a war for her.... Fighting ...Guns, killing people, bombs, all this was new and the thought of this concerned him.

Denise concerned him. All their plans. Their dreams of going to America, marrying, a family... What to do?

Chapter 4

Some things I'm not sure about,
Like what is right and what is wrong,
I guess at my age, I'm just a ding dong,
I just want to help the world,
I just want to help my friends,
I would like to see all the wars end,
May be I'll get the chance,
When I'm older I will see,
What it is meant to be...for me.

A Sign, a Poster...

The streets were crowed as he walked brushing shoulders with people he did not know. Children were playing in the streets. Tall buildings surrounded him. They seemed to look at him as he walked. A man sat beside of a building. He had no legs but a big smile as he held out his hands.

"Kind sir, maybe a little change."

David rubbed his legs and handed the man some money.

"Merci kind sir."

It was as if God were talking to him.

Slowly David moved into the crowd again. The man with no legs was the answer. He knew then what he must do. He must help. He must go to war. He must fight for Denise, Paris, and what he believed in.

A tall building made of dark stone called to him. As he stood in front of it, the large poster gloomed at him. The poster was of a picture of children playing. Two people dressed in the blue uniform of the French Air Force held the children in their hands.

The caption said something that he had felt before.... "We are there for you."

David smiled as he climbed the stairs to the double doors. This is what he must do… This was the answer… The large brown door with the letters; "Join" went through his mind. A man in uniform sat reading the newspaper as David knocked and opened the door. "Hello there."

There again was a poster on the wall. "We are there for you."

"Hi, I'm David Hunt and would like some information about signing up for service."

The Captain looked startled. "You are American right?"

"Yes sir I am." The Captain stood. "Please have a seat, let us talk about this. Hunt, are you the son of the American that is working at the Embassy?"

"Yes sir, my father was transferred here over two years ago."

The Captain smiled and sat on the desk. "I have had the pleasure of meeting him. It is an honor to meet you. But I am confused, as an American, why do you want to join our service?"

"Well sir, as the poster says, I am here to help."

"Well I am very pleased to hear you want to help France. We don't have many Americans in our troops but we can use all the help we can get. What do you want I mean how do you want to help France?"

"Fly sir. Aircraft is my life. I have been flying since I was nine years old. My father taught me everything about flying and I would love to fly for France."

The Captain stood and took papers from his desk.

"That is something that we need. You will have to be schooled in our ways to fly. It will take courage and most of all we will be proud for you to serve in the Air France Service. Good luck to you David Hunt. Do you have any questions about the France or the school or our ways of flying?"

"Not now but I am sure there are many things that I don't know about but want to learn how I can be the best airman you have. As far as to France, I have grown to love the people here and plan to stay here."

"That will make you a good airman and pilot. France is lucky to have you here to I'm sure. Again, good luck to you Mr. Hunt."

David stood outside of the building looking at the forms that he had been given. This was his first step in giving back to France and his dream of flying. The next step was to get his father's help. Denise also went through his mind but how to tell her was going to be a little touchy.

Chapter 5

I think I'm right, I could be wrong,
I asked my mother what I should do,
Her answer came out of the blue,
"You are too young to understand,
Wait till you're a grown man,
Then you will see what life about."
Guess I will wait and hope to see,
What is really ahead of me...?

I Must Go and Be There.

David lay in bed reading the forms and application. He knew that his father would help with the paperwork. It seemed simple, just fill it out, go to school, wear the uniform and fly a plane. Maybe I could just take supplies to the troupes or food to the hungry. Sure, there are all kinds of ways to help.

He lay there thinking about Denise and what she would say. A chuckle came to him. "She will be proud of me." He rolled over looking at her picture on the stand. "For you my Angel, for you and France."

David also remembered when he was almost seventeen when he received the news. It was a cool evening in Washington. The fire in the fireplace was bright. His mother was in the kitchen doing this and that when his father came in the house. As he took off his overcoat and hung is on the brass coat rack he called out, "I'm home, everybody gather around." As the three of them sat in the living room his dad opened his briefcase, took some papers out, and excitedly waved them in the air.

"Guess what? We are moving to Paris France. My transfer came in."

I was stunned. Mother clapped her hands. They had always wanted to go there.

"But dad, what about my school? My flying lessons? All of my friends?"

"Son, you can continue flying lessons there and the private schools there are the best. Best of all, the French girls will love you."

And two months later they were on their way to Paris France.

The sound of his name came from the hallway. He stood looking at the papers.

"David, dinner is ready."

As he walked down the stairs he put the papers in his pants pocket. As he entered the dining room his father waved at him. "Hey son, bet you didn't think I was here and by the way, got news for you. Sit down, sit down."

Mrs. Hunt came out carrying a tray of chicken.

She put it in front of David and kissed his head. "You and your father's favorite." It was a great time for all. They did not spend time together that much with Mr. Hunt at the Embassy. The duties there kept him there almost all the time.

Now was time that they always looked forward to. The smells of the food was amazing. Soon Mrs. Hunt stood and went to the kitchen.

David sat thinking about what he was about to do.

Slowly he drank the wine. His father started to stand.

"No wait dad. I need to talk to you."

"Alright son, there is something to tell you to. Let me go first. Son, I have great news. We can go back to

America soon. How about that? My transfer came thru. We can go home."

David sat in shock. Quickly he downed the wine.

"We what? Dad, what are you saying?"

"Just that, we can go back to America. Isn't that what you have been wanting?"

David stood and walked around the table and sat by his father. Slowly he handed the papers to him.

"What is this?" He opened the papers and looked at David. "You can't be serious? David, we talked about the war, but son you should think this over. This is a big step. You are an American."

David hit the table and looked at his father. "I have thought it all over and this is what I want to do. You said you would help me so I need your help. Dad, I thought you and mom would be pleased and proud of me."

Mr. Hunt stood shaking his head. He went to the bay windows looking at the sky. The sky was filled with darkness. He stood thinking of what was to come. The war was coming and he knew it.

"What about you and Denise? She was coming too. Son, son, my son, we love you very much but if that is your wish, I will help you anyway I can." He put the papers in his suit coat and walked out of the room.

"Will you dad, will you help me?"

Time stood still. David had one last thing to do. He must tell Denise.

A cool breeze blew across the land making the tall grass rock slowly. He sat throwing stones into the small stream. Denise stood by the tall tree watching him. The smell of flowers she had picked tickled her nose.

Slowly she walked to him. She let the flowers fall over his head and laughed. He reached for a flower without looking at her. She unbuttons a few buttons on her dress and sat down beside him. "David, why are you so pensive? Are your thoughts not of me?"

David dropped his head. "They are only of you. They are only of us. I love you very much, but there is something I must tell you."

"This is not like you David. What is wrong?"

David turned to her and touched her face.

"It is nothing that is wrong, it's, well, I must do something you may not like. I have been thinking about you and France and my life. The war is only a short time away, maybe a year or two." He thought about his father.

"My father says that Germany will attack Paris. Denise I want you to go to America with them. You will be safe."

"David, this is my country. Would you leave your country if it were at war? Nor would I... I love you.... Will you fight for Paris? Will you be safe here? Will you die for France? Why must you do this?"

"Sweetheart, I don't know if I will even be in the war. I just want to fly a plane and help the troupes. There are so many things I can do to help. Let's take one step at a time, okay."

She laid her head in his lap looking up at him. "Do you have a plan?"

He brushed her hair. "Well yes and no. Dad is going to help me with joining the Air Force and flying school, but from there I don't know. If, and I say if, there is a war you should go to America. Then I will follow later."

"David we talked about this. I will never leave France. I will wait for you here. We must never be apart." She hit his arm hard. "You understand me? We must never we be apart."

Time…. Time… time…

It was a matter of time as weeks and months went by. The news of a possible war was the talk of Paris. All David could think about was flying a plane for France as he entered the gates of the base.

David stood in front of a desk as a Captain read David's papers.

"I see you are the son of Mr. Hunt. He is a fine man. I know him well. You know there will be a lot of work ahead of you. Tell me David, why do you want to join the French Air Force? You are an American."

David stood at attention. "Sir, I want to serve France. I have been here well over two years and have learned to love the people and the land. I consider this as my home. Yes sir, I am an American, but I am here and want to serve the people and France."

David smiled and thought back to the days of flying. "Since I was a small boy, I have studied aviation and have flown small aircraft, studied flight plans, instrument training, skies, clouds, and have passed the test for my pilot's license. I feel that I can learn to fly aircrafts that will help in the war to come if needed. Sir, I am ready to learn and serve."

"Well Mr. Hunt, you may get the chance. First, there is Officer's school. There I will assign you to learn and fly aircrafts that will be of service to us. As you know this is not a short course." He again looked at the papers. "Also, you may not be a part of the war. You will be under my command."

"Sir, I will be pleased to be a part of your command. Sir, I would also be pleased to fight at your service. Sir, please do not give me special attention because of my father."

The Captain stood and laughed. "I am glad to see you are your own man. I am pleased to see you want to serve France. I am pleased to have an American in my command. Now, you will be notified when and where to report to. I suppose that I can call you Lieutenant Hunt, after you pass training."

"Thank you sir, I will pass all of my training, thank you sir."

David was now Lieutenant Hunt, almost.

David left the office with his head held high. All of Paris looked different to him. He felt part of something special. The people looked at him and waved. How did they know? As he walked the streets he could see himself as a Frenchman. He was now a part of a new country and the French Air force. American yes but he knew that his duty was now to help France and serve the best he could. This was his destiny to fly and to make his mother and father proud of him. Denise would also be proud of him. He wanted now to wear the uniform of the French Air Force. He wanted to wear the silver bars on his uniform. He wanted to be Lieutenant David Hunt. All time and years as a young boy was now paying off when he was putting airplanes together. All the flying lessons his dad had given to him and all the test that he had to pass was now putting him where he wanted to be.

Chapter 6

I'm pretty smart for a kid of eight,
Sometimes okay, sometimes great,
But one thing I learned at school,
If you study real hard,
You aren't a fool,
My grades are high and getting better,
My friends think I'm crazy,
And I wonder why,
All I want is to fly,
Like a bird, but in a plane,
Is that unreal, is that insane?

Home Sweet Home

The sky was never as clear as he lay in his bed looking out of the window. Visions of himself flying. His mind raced with thoughts of Denise, his mother and dad. What would they say? He reached for the picture of Denise. He kissed and held it to his heart. "You understand. We will be together always. Yes, I love you baby, I really do. This is the beginning of something new for us."

David bounced down the stairs shouting. "Mother, got something to tell you... Mother..."

Mrs. Hunt sat in the living room reading. He ran to her and fell at her feet. "I did it mother, I did it."

She put her book down and took off her glasses. "What did you do now? Pass a test?"

He waved his hands. "Mother I have joined the French Air Force. With dad's help I am now in. Aren't you proud of me? I am a Lieutenant, almost."

Mrs. Hunt hit him with the book. "You are crazy that is what you are."

"Today, I signed up and will be reporting soon. Wait till dad hears the news."

She pushed him off and stood. "But we have plans to go home. America is where you belong not here and not in some Air Force. Your father has worked hard for all of us to go home, even to take Denise so you and she can live in America."

David stood and walked around the room. "You don't understand. I want this. I want to serve France. I love this country... and Denise, well we have already talked about this. She wants to stay here. You and dad can go and in time we will come to America. That is our plan."

"David, son, give it some more thought. This is not the life for you two. Home is where you and Denise should have children. A home and a good life. If you want to serve something, serve America."

"I will mother, in a few years. Then Denise and I will come home. Raise a family, buy a house, live the good life, but for now, this is the right thing to do. Mother, this is something I want to do."

She stormed out of the room. David felt bad that she did not understand. He sat with his head in his hands.

He thought of what his dad would say. He knew that he would approve. He hoped Denise would to...

A New Life...

"And then what happened?" She walked to him as he read the newspaper.

"Well, she was not very happy. All she could say was America is your home. I think dad will convince her that this is the right thing to do... Wow, look at this. A one large bedroom apartment near the Embassy, and not too far from the base. What do you think? Let's go take a look at it."

"David are you sure about all this? I mean she may be right."

He read more. "First floor, kitchen, it is perfect for us. Come on, let's go now and take a look."

It was a perfect place as they walked around making plans where things should go. David stood in the doorway looking down the street. "Look Denise, you can see the Embassy about six blocks from here."

She came and rapped her arms around him as he pointed to the tall building. "Yep, that's it. So, tell me, what do you think?"

She kissed his ear and whispered. "I like the bedroom."

"Huh, me to, want to break it in?" The best part of the day was making love.

Denise started gathering her clothes. "You are a great lover but one thing don't you think we should buy a bed?"

The rest of the day was spent shopping for things.

Duty Calls...

Mr. Hunt read David's papers. David stood waiting for his response. "Well everything seems to be in order. You have been assigned to flight school and officers training. Better get your things in order because you have a lot to do. You know David, I am proud of you. You made a decision and followed through with it. Your mother might not agree with things but I do. So, I wish you the best of things to come. You are a good man. I am proud to be your father." They stood hugging each other.

"Thanks dad for everything. You know, this may not be such a bad war after all. And when it is over Denise and I will come home and get you to help us there."

"You got it son, and I heard that it will not even be a war. Paris is an open and free city. France does not want to fight. Besides, they have America and England to stand with them. The Germans do not have a chance. So, Mr. Lieutenant Hunt, just go and have fun and be safe."

David sat hearing his father's words echoing in his head. "So Mr. Lieutenant Hunt, go have fun and be safe. The Germans do not have a chance."

"You're right dad. Just have fun and be safe. Thanks dad."

David was very excited about the talk with his father. The idea of flying and being a Lieutenant was now his dream come true. The other part was that there might not even be a war and the best of all was the thought of him and Denise going back to America after his tour of duty. There they could have a great life with a family, a house and a dog. He laughed thinking about a dog and what to name their kids. David Jr. would be nice and if a girl, well the name of Denise would be wonderful or they could call her, Denny or maybe Jean. Yeah, that's French, yeah.

Chapter 7

I pray every night God hear my prayer,
Watch over me from head to feet,
Now I lay me down to sleep,
If I should die before I wake,
I pray the Lord my soul to take,
God bless mother and dad,
And if I should die don't make them sad,
For they are the best a kid ever had.

Easy Going...

It was as David had done all this in another life.

He sat at the computer taking a simulator class on the aircraft that he would fly. The obsession to fly was always on his mind. Superman could fly, so he wanted to fly to. At five years old was his first attempt to fly but the towel around his neck and his opened arms did not work. Only a sprained waist and a small cut on his knee came from the jump from the fence. It was then that model planes came into his life. His father brought home two different types of planes in their boxes and handed them to David.

"Tell you what son, you put these planes together and learn about them and one day I will teach you how to fly."

At six years old, David had built thirty-two different types of aircrafts. At seven years old his father took him to the private airport for his first close up experience with a real airplane.

David was a quick study. As he and his father sat in the small plane, he touched everything as his father would ask him, "What is this...What does this do." At eight, David had read books about air currents, air speeds, clouds, sun, stars, rain, and knew the instrument panels very well.

It was David's tenth birthday. Sitting across the breakfast table, Mr. Hunt leaned back in his chair with a smile.

"Well David, how would you like to fly today?"

David lit up like a thirty-two foot Christmas tree.

"You mean off the ground?"

"Yep, I have a plane reserved for us today." Mr. Hunt had been flying for many years and now it was time for David to show what he had learned.

David stood up with his arms out stretched and flew around the table making plane noises.

"Hey, sit down, think you can do it?"

David sat thinking. "I think so, but I will need your help landing."

"You will need more than that son. You must get the feel of everything and most of all you must stay in touch with yourself. Remember, feel everything and touch everything."

"Yes sir, feel and touch, feel everything, touch everything."

The classroom was quiet. David could feel his heart beating as his breath came fast. David's hands roamed all over the simulator panel touching everything. His mind could feel his body come to life with excitement. "Yes sir, feel, and touch."

The Captain stepped to him. "You say something?"

David smiled… "No sir."

Things were different for him as the plane turned circles, dives, climbs, rolls, and touch and go. Then there was a fighter plane on his tail. He then had to get away fast. The simulator fighter was firing rockets at him.

One hit the wing sending him in a downward spin. David lost it. He had never thought that his plane would be hit or in trouble. Captain James stood watching as David tried to avoid a crash. David did his best but the plane crashed. "Well Lieutenant, you just died. Got some work to do huh."

He sat with his head in his hands. "Yes sir, lot of work to do. Tell me sir, what would you have done?"

The Captain laughed. "First, I would call and reported my position. Then they could come and get me. Then I would bale out of the plane. But you should know that that jet has rockets and know how to avoid them. You will learn Lieutenant. You had better learn or you will die for real."

David sat looking at the computer. A lesson well learned. The test started again.

David thought what the Captain had said. The flying was the easy part. What he had to learn was how to save his ass.

At 50,000 feet three jet fighters came out of the blue firing at him. He knew that his choice was to go high or dive below them. He froze. The jets began to get closer to him. All of a sudden his plane started to roll.

David started his climb. Rolling higher and higher at a speed he had never done before. At the top of his climb he started a roll downward. Faster and faster the plane plunged to earth. As he went in a tailspin he saw the planes ahead of him. His hands grabbed the stick and his thumb pressed on the guns of his plane. Fire and flames shot from the guns. His eyes were on the instrument panel.

There was a plane in his view. The guns roared as they fired. The fighter was hit. Smoke poured as it went down. He quickly circled looking for the other two planes.

Again he went high in the sky and started his dive again. There they were. They split up, one going high and one low. David started a roll down and called on the radio. "Need help!" A jet fell in behind him and started firing.

David pulled the plane in a circle roll and came in behind the fighter jet. He had the fighter in his sights. The jet did a roll and so did David, firing all the way. The fighter was hit and went out of sight as smoke trailed in the sky. The fight was over. David had won.

The simulator showed the jet fighter had retreated. David fell back in the seat. All the training had paid off. He sat thinking about the simulator.

This was for training. What would have happen if this was for real. David's legs shook as he stood up. He thought about if he could cut it if it were for real. This one he had won. What about the next one?

Death was something he had never come in contact with… Death was real… He thought of Denise and their love for each other. He thought about his mother and her wanting him to come home to America.

He heard his father saying, "I'm proud of you son." Then he thought about the fighter jets firing at him. Now was the time to make another decision about all of this. He stood looking at the computer. This was a test but in the real world that was another thing. Even after all this training, was this, the right thing for him to do? Would it be alright just to go home with Denise and call all this the end? What the hell to do? All he knew was he could not quite. He was a fighter and this was a fight to the finish.

Chapter 8

It doesn't take long to learn a song,
Just learn the words and play along,
And the more you sing the better you get,
It takes time to get it right,
But once you learn you won the fight,
And that is life, as I see things now,
To do what you want to do,
You can win or lose but you must try...

Something is wrong...

As night fell David stood in the doorway of the apartment. He watched the lights of the city blinking. As he stood there he thought of the jet fighters and the battle they had had. The sounds of the jets, the firing of the guns, the plane being hit. His plane crashing. Was it a test for him or was it a test of what might be. He could hear the Captain saying, "Your dead." He kept asking himself, "Is this what I really want to do?"

Denise came up behind him. "What did you say?"

David spun around and grabbed her.

"Oh baby baby, I love you so much. I thought about you all day. What would I do without you? Today in class things made me see that you are my life." He touched her cheek. "And I would die for you."

She saw in his face that something was bothering him. She took his hand and placed it on her heart.

"I love you too much. Can you feel my love beating for you? If I can see your pain, I will take it from you. Now I see you troubled and it bothers me. Will you tell me of it?"

He touched her chin and kissed her. "It happened in class. There was a simulator of planes in a fight. They shot me down. There was nothing I could do... They killed me...All I could do was think about you. What would you do if I were killed? What if mother was right? Should we go to America and forget about all this? I could fly for an airline company and be happy there. We don't need this war. Am I right or wrong?"

"What does your heart tell you? Does it say, run? Does it say to you that you care of people? David, I do not want to leave here but if you think we should go, I will be happy with you anywhere you are. Time will pass and all will be well. God will watch over us. You are a strong man, and I trust you in your decision."

A feeling ran through him. He looked into the sky. "You know, you are right. My heart says that life is a wonderful thing and I know what to do. I will be the best pilot that France ever had. I will serve this country and make you proud of me. I will always have you by my side, always. I will never die. This I promise you. You will have me forever."

"Now, what do you say about us going out for dinner, and then we will make love all night"

David laughed. "And we will make love all night."

The white wine made the fish a great meal. Denise held up her glass.

"I want to make a toast. A toast to the small things in life, a toast to France, a toast to you and to me that we never part and toast to the stars that they may forever see our love. I love you David Hunt." Their glasses touched. Their arms closed around each other. Their eyes met.

"And I love you Denise Val Jean. I also have a toast. May you always guide me through the darkness and together we will find the light. May your love for me be as strong as my love is for you." David reached in his jacket pocket. "There is more. May you accept this ring as I accept you forever. Will you marry me? Someday?"

Tears of joy filled her eyes as he slipped the ring on her finger. She began to cry. "Yes David, yes. I will marry you, someday."

Two girls sat at a table laughing. One of the girls pointed at Denise and David.

"I dare you."

"Oh I will alright." She stood and slowly walked to the table. Denise looked up at her.

"Hi Denise, are you having fun?" Denise knew her from one of her classes and did not like her.

"Oh, hi, as a matter of fact, we are."

"Why don't you introduce me to your friend?"

Denise looked to David. "David, this is a girl from school, sorry what is your name?"

The girl smiled and held out her hand. "Hi, I'm Susan. Denise, he has strong hands and is very handsome. You are American right?"

"Hi and yes thank you."

"Denise, do you mind if I join you two?"

"We were just leaving."

"Oh silly girl don't leave, I want to talk to David." Susan started to sit.

Denise stood and looked to David. "Are you ready to go?"

David stood. "Guess so."

Susan moved close to David. "Wow, tall, dark, strong and very good looking. Tell me David, do you like French women? They say we are great lovers."

David smiled and looked at Denise. "Yes, and I have the best lover."

Susan took his hand. "If you want a real French lover, you should call me."

Denise's hand hit a glass of wine on the table, and it fell off and spilled all over Susan's feet. Susan drew back to slap her. David grabbed her hand. Denise moved to her. They stood eye to eye.

"Let her go. If she wants to fight me, I will show you how French I am. You want to fight with me Susan?"

Susan kicked the glass on the floor. She stared at Denise. "Not this time, I might win and take your boyfriend away from you."

David smiled at her. "You can't take anything away from Denise, especially me. Let's go baby."

Denise smiled at David.

They stood outside of the restaurant. David held her tight. "Wow, you are something else."

"What do you mean something else?"

"The way you handled her. You were ready to fight for me."

Denise kissed him. "You are worth fighting for. Besides she would not have won. I am very strong." They laughed and laughed.

Best of Times...

Everything was perfect and going well. The apartment was now finished and in order.

Denise had given the place atmosphere with lace curtains, flowers, plants, and a fish bowl with three small fish swimming around.

David sat as a desk doing his homework and occasionally glanced at Denise lying on the couch reading a French book of poems.

It was a quiet evening as soft music sounds of the Glenn Miller Orchestra drifted from the radio. Slowly she strolled over to him and sits on the desk.

She watched as his left hand wrote answers on the page. She pointed to an answer he had answered. "Are you sure about that? I mean the spelling."

He looked at the answer. "You're right it should be country, not counrty. Thank God it's almost finished. A little more history and I'll be through with all this high school stuff and on to the big stuff."

"You mean Officer's school and your flying classes."

"Yep, Captain says that I am doing well."

She lay across the desk and shyly smiled. "That's not all your good at." She unbuttoned her shirt top and exposed her firm breast.

David closed his books and pushed them aside. A boyish smile came as he caressed her breast.

He leaned and kissed her large nipples. His hand slid into her jeans as his fingers found her pubic hairs and her wetness. "Take me to bed David, take me." His strong arms wrapped around her as he picked her up.

It was about to be a night of passion and love.

School is out...almost...

Twenty-six Frenchman and David sat in the class. The room was very quiet as the Captain walked down the aisle passing out papers face down on their desks. He went to the chalkboard and wrote in large letters.

Everyone watched as he wrote the last letter on the board, "D". He turned and smiled. "Today, we all should be proud to have an American in our country. Today, it is the first time in my life that an American is part of the French Air Force." He smiled at David. "Yes, there have been others, but I am pleased to have Lieutenant David Hunt under my command. Lieutenant Hunt, would you step up here."

David's legs shook as he stood. Slowly he looked at all his class members and walked to the desk where the Captain stood. "Sir."

"David I guess you are wondering why I did not give you papers. Well I personally wanted to hand these to you in front of all of these men a gift for all your hard work. Lieutenant Hunt, I congratulate you as you have passed with high honors your High School Diploma."

Everyone stood and applauded and shouted David's name. He could not believe that it was over. All the studying and hours of research were now in his hand. He stood looking at the diploma.

Now his father and mother would be the first to see this. Now the larger picture was clear. He could see Denise and the life ahead of them. The Captain reached for his hand. The sound of his name was even louder as David shook the Captain's hand.

"Congratulations David, now the real test begins."

The Real Test Starts…. Now,

The restaurant and smell of French food filled the table as Mr. and Mrs. Hunt and Denise raised their glasses in a salute to David. His father spoke first.

"Son, there has been times that I have been happy, but never any more than now." His father continued.

"We, your mother and I, knew you were always a special child. A dreamer. A boy that always wanted more. Now we see a man in front of us. Thank you David for making us so happy."

His mother squeezed his hand and kissed him. "We love you son."

Denise stood with glass in hand. "I would like to say to you David that you have also made me very happy. You have given me many things but mostly you have given me hope, your heart and dreams, and your love, Merci." She sat as David stood.

"Merci tress beaucoup, it is you that I salute. You have stood by me when I needed you to understand that I must do things that may or may not be as others would do. I amour you very much… And to you, Mother, thank you for giving me all your guidance and love and wisdom. Father, what can I say? If it weren't for you all this would not have come true. You have inspired me, given me the chance to prove that I can be a man. Both of you have let me grow and to me, that is what life is all about… Growing…Now, I must grow even more." He raised his glass.

"Now, there is a world that Denise and I must go into. This will be a world of France and a large world of America. I know that Denise and I will go and prevail in both worlds. I do with all my heart want to thank you all for standing by me… merci."

Mrs. Hunt reached for Mr. Hunt's hand. "It's getting late hon, let's go and leave these young lovers to talk."

Mr. Hunt squeezed her hand. "You're right, it is late. Okay you two enjoy your evening and David we will talk later."

Denise and David watched as they left the restaurant. Denise giggled. "She called us lovers."

Chapter 9

It's hard to say goodbye to your friends,
And things you love and the blue sky above,
But all good things must come to an end,
We are taught this by the ways of Zen,
To love and to protect are the way of life,
To honor and serve will bring happiness,
To your soul and will make your life hold…
As a child I have learned this way,
To love and cherish will make my day,
And all through my life,
Love will show me the way.

Flying Higher than Ever...

It took several weeks of serious training to get it right. The simulator class of flying was an exciting way of learning. Flying high in circles and dives and climbs and the force of the G's as the plane soared through the air was amazing. The feel of the stick in his hand could make all his dreams come true. As he rolled the plane and climbed straight up into the heavens he thought of Denise sitting in back of him. They together could explore the skies and visit with God. Now, he must be the best he could be. All of a sudden, three fighters were all around him. Guns began to fire. He had been hit. Smoke poured from his plane. The instruments began to flash. All his training came to him as he flipped switches to control the fire and smoke.

The Captain stood behind him watching as David started his roll and cut one of the jets.

David started to dive. "Mayday, Mayday, I have been hit." The G forces were blinding as he looked to see the smoke began to disappear. The land and ocean below began to get closer and closer.

With a quick pull on the stick the plane began to pull to a level as he looked at the panel. "Very nice David."

David did not respond only continued to control the plane. Now what went through his mind.

The plane was now under control and still had speed to land, climb, or David could bail out. He still had fight in him as he pulled back on the stick and began to climb back to the sky. There they were.

Three fighters waiting high in the sky. Now it was his turn to fight. The panel showed a plane in sight. He smiled as his thumb pressed the button on the stick.

The guns began to fire a stream of firing bullets. The fighter was hit and smoke filled the air as it fell. The two fighters began to retreat. David had won this battle.

Smoke again came from his plane. David called the base that he was coming in for a landing. The exercise was over. "I would not have done that David. You were on fire and the plane was in danger." David turned to him. "Sir, all the instruments told me that I was safe to continue the flight. I am here to do what I think is best."

The Captain laughed. "No son, you are here to learn not to do as you please, but I must say, well done."

Night of Tears...

They stood outside their apartment talking. David's hands and arms waved in the air. "They were coming from everywhere. I was hit. That's when I decided to go down. Then I thought, go get them." He looked for her reaction. Denise stood and walked to the window. A tear came to her face. Another tear came.

She looked into the dark night. "I will lose you." She turned to him. "I will lose you." He came to her with opened arms and a smile.

"Baby, it was an exercise. It was a test, it was not real. You know something, all the time I was thinking of you. You and I were flying high in the heavens holding God's hand."

"And did God tell you to act foolish? Did he?"

David lay asleep as Denise stood looking at him. She went to the window and fell to her knees. The stars in the heavens blinked through the darkness. She put her hands together in prayer and closed her eyes.

"My God, hear my thoughts. I love him so much. Show him this... Show him I must not lose him..."

She slowly opened her eyes. Tears began to roll down her face. "Show me he will be with you. Please protect him, protect him please here me" She began to cry more. She stood and again looked at David sleeping. Slowly she wiped the tears and sit on the bed looking at him.

"You are everything to me... You are my life..."

With her soft smile she laid her head on his arm and soon was sleeping.

Chapter 10

Fear of the unknown is worst feeling of all,
It will make us kneel it will make us crawl,
It will make us love the things that are dear,
There is nothing worse than unknown fear,
The big guys in school shake their fist in my face,
And I pray for wisdom and grace,
But I know in the end when all is done,
A blue sky will appear and so will the sun…
So fear can't touch me for love will prevail,
So go away fear, … Go to hell.

Bye Mother, I will see you later...

Mr. Hunt opened his desk draw and put a stack of papers away. David sat watching him. Slowly his father turned to him.

"Well son, I hate to say this but the war is getting closer and closer. I am sending your mother back to the States. She will be leaving soon. I have been ordered to leave myself. My concern is you."

David sat in shock. "When did you find all this out? You mean the Germans are going to attack Paris? But why they can't win."

"No they can't, but all reports say they will attack. The question is, when. I also think for the safety of Denise that she should go to."

David shook his head. "That is out of the question. She will never leave. This is her home. We knew this might happen and we have plans to go after the so-called war is over. When is mother leaving? When will you leave?"

"She will leave in a few days. Me, I have things to do before I need to leave. Son, you need to talk to Denise about this. She will be safer if she were to leave. No one knows just what is going to happen or when."

David stood and walked around the room. "Do you think this is really going to be a real war?"

Mr. Hunt tapped his pen on the desk. "War, no, but it will harm a lot of people. Hitler is a crazy man.

I think his Army will hit and run. That is the way they do things."

David hit the desk. He looked at his father. "France will fight. America will fight. The English will fight. There is no way the Germans can win this."

"You are right son that is why I want to just be safe and get your mother and Denise out of the way of any danger. Now, your mother and I want you and Denise to come over for dinner and to talk about all this. Say, Tuesday night?"

"Well if you think it would help but she is not going to leave Paris…Tell me dad, would you leave America if it happens there."

America...

Dishes rattled in the sink as Denise and Mrs. Hunt stood quietly passing things. Dinner had been quiet with no mention of the war or leaving. David and his father sat in the large living room playing chess.

Even they were quiet. David picked up the King and just starred at it. Mr. Hunt leaned back in his chair. "Well?"

Slowly, David laid the piece down on its side. "You win dad."

A smile came with words of wisdom. "Son, sometimes you win, sometimes you wish you had never played the game. You always have a choice."

"You're talking about my choice aren't you? Dad, even you know I am right."

The kitchen door swung open and Mrs. Hunt and Denise came in laughing. "She is going to make you very happy David. I love this girl."

They sat in silence looking at each other. Mr. Hunt went to the bookshelf and took a book from it. He turned to them and flipped through the pages. Slowly he came back to his chair. "History has taught us that things repeat themselves. Wars that have been have given us direction into the future. Things that we should do and things we should not do. To retreat is a value of life. I say all this because it is best for your mother to go back to a safe place. I also think Denise should go to. Denise, I know you will not and I honor your decision."

Mr. Hunt continued. "So, with that said, your mother will be leaving soon to go back to America. I, too, have been ordered to, retreat."

David reached for Denise's hand. "Mother, I don't know what is going to happen here, but we love you too much to see you stay in any danger. We want you to go. Denise and I will come to you and dad when this is over. Mother, we know what we must do and father is right."

Denise reached for Mrs. Hunt's hand. "It is best for you to leave. What we ask for is for you to pray for us. This is my land and home and I must stay and help in any way I can, but you must leave. We love you very much."

David held back tears. He moved to the couch and put his arms around her. "I love you mom that is why you must go."

Mrs. Hunt began to cry. She hugged him and whispered. "I know you do, and I know your father is right. I will go, but my heart will be here with both of you." She ran her hands through his hair. "You are my son."

It is over...

David stood looking in the mirror at his self. He was proud of the uniform that he wore.

The bars on his shirt and a star on his chest were a symbol of what he had wanted. Denise stood as he looked at her in the mirror.

"Well, what do you think about your man?"

She came to him and touched the silver bar on his uniform. "I am very proud of you. I see a man that I love and respect. I see a man that will do anything for me, to fight for what is right, to fight for my country, to be my lover always."

He put his hat on and turned to hold her. "Always my love, always. Okay, I am ready. Today, I am a flyer for the French Air Force. All my training is over, and I am ready. Today, I fly high in the sky all by myself."

Denise laughed. "Will you wave to me when you fly over my head? I will wave back to you... David, please be careful."

"Baby, I love you too much not to be careful. This is what I have been dreaming of."

"This is what we both have dreamed of and my prayer is with you."

"Not to worry, this is just a flying test, I'll be just fine."

"Don't forget to wave to me, I will stand by the door waiting for you."

"Honey you are in my every thoughts and I will wave to you."

She watched as he ran down the street to the base. "Love you."

Chapter 11

It feels good when the storm has passed,
The sky turns blue at last at last,
The rain has cleared the air.
But I wonder if God meant it to be,
For the ocean to be calm and so the sea.
For I love everything,
And everything loves me.
But if it should rain again and I'm sure,
To say, the sun and sky will be pure,
I will go on the best I can,
For all good things must come to an end,
And I will be my own man.

The High Ride...

They lay in bed as David excitedly told her the story of the sounds of the jet as he took off. He waved his hands and made the motion of the plane as it went up.

His eyes were big as he felt the thrust of the jet as it went higher and higher. All his training came to him as he pulled back on the stick. His hands showed her how the jet rolled as it climbed into the heavens. He sits up in the bed and looked at her. "Never, have I felt that way."

She smiled and a small laugh came to her. "Not even when we make love?"

His eyes searched her body. His hands wandered over her large breast. The thoughts of the jet had been replaced. He kissed her nipples as his hand wandered between her legs. Her breathing became faster as she pulled his head to her breast.

Slowly he moved on top of her. Her eyes closed as they began to make love. "Oh yes David, love me hard." His movements made her cry for more as he held her tight. Passion was more that she could stand as she pulled his body deeper into her. Deeper, faster, harder, made her throw her head from side to side. He became stronger as he began to come in her body. Her screams came loud as she began to climax. Her body shook as she cried out in the night of pleasure. He fell on her breathing fast. They kissed deeply as their hearts beat fast.

He fell to her side still holding her hand. "Wow."

She rolled to him with her hand rubbing his chest. "I say, Wow too. I say you are a wonderful lover. You take me to the heavens."

It was a short sleep for them. Suddenly, the sounds of sirens sounded through the city. The roar and rumble in the night fog woke them. David ran to the window looking into the dark sky. Flashes of small lights from six ME-109 fighters led the way for two Junker Ju 87 Bombers. The building shook as the German planes flew overhead. Denise ran to David. They held each other as the awesome sound shook pictures from the walls.

Suddenly, time stood still. Silence filled the air. Only a slight rumble of the passing planes drifted into the night.

"David what was that? What just happened?"

He held her tight as he looked into the darkness. He could feel her heart pounding. Her eyes searched his. Slowly he kissed her forehead as he whispered to her.

"Nothing to be afraid of, just a recon patrol, they are gone now."

"Were they German planes? Why were they here?"

He took her back to the bed as they sat down. "To scare us, that is their way. Just to put fear in us, then they go away."

"And then what?"

"Sweetheart, we are safe. Paris is strong and safe. Nothing will happen, I promise."

Denise lay back on the bed with outstretched arms. "Hold me David, hold me forever."

What must be done?

The news was full of the surprise. One paper said, "Paris is at war."…. The radio said, "It is an attack on France."

The air base was on full alert with planes standing by ready to fight. Television stations had tape of the German planes that was shown all that day. Phones at the Embassy did not stop ringing. All of Europe wanted to know how did this happen and why.

The tapping of the Captain's cane on the desk drew everyone's attention. "Gentlemen, this was a preview of things to come. From now on we have orders to fly day and night. Six aircraft will be in the air at all times. Shifts will be set. All pilots and crews will remain on duty and stay on the base starting now. You will not speak to any media about this mission. Your assignments will be posted within the hour. Are there any questions?"

A young man raised his hand and stood. "Sir, were we under attack?"

The Captain laughed. "Son, if we had been under an attack we would all be dead. No we were not. We were asleep. We expected this to happen months from now. Now gentlemen, we are awake." The Captain rapped hard on the desk.

"We are thirty-six of the best trained pilots in this squadron and there are more than seventy-two squadrons plus the Americans and the English planes. Yes gentlemen we are awake now, any more questions? Dismissed."

David sat tapping his pen on the desktop. Thoughts of the night filled his mind. He could still feel Denise's heart beating and see the fear in her eyes. He could still hear the sounds of the planes in the night. Small lights blinked in his mind.

"Lieutenant Hunt, is there something on your mind?"

David looked at him as if he were not there.

"David?"

"Ah, no sir, sir are you married?"

"Yes for twenty-two years, why?"

"Sir, what does your wife think about you and the war?"

The Captain walked to him and sat down. "She loves me and has lots of confidence in what I do."

"Does she ever want the two of you to be just... two people?"

"David son, we are just two people. So happens that I am in the Air Force and love my country."

"Thank you sir, mind if I sit here awhile?"

The Captain stood and went to the door, turned and looked at David. "If you ever want to talk about anything, I am here. Close the door when you leave."

The door slowly closed.

David opened his pad and began to write. His voice mumbled words.

"Dearest Denise, I love you. Ever since we met I knew that we were meant for each other. I breathe your breath and feel every emotion you have. We are two people in this world, but I know you are the special one in my life and will always be. If we should ever part, I want you to know that you will still be with me always. I will come to you again in your dreams, in your heart, for I am in your soul, and you are in my soul. Together we will fight, and we will prevail. Life, wars, floods, and dark skies will never keep us apart... for we are strong. We have what no others have... We have each other... no matter what... We have each other always..."

The one that loves you very much,
David

He sat looking at the words on the paper. He kissed the paper and folded it. In the desk drawer was an envelope. He put the paper in it and sealed it with a kiss. "I will love you always no matter what happens."

Sam a French pilot stood in the doorway as David started to leave. "Wait a minute Hunt. I want to talk to you."

"Sure, what about?"

"You think you are a hotshot pilot don't you. Well I have news for you. You're nothing but a coward an American coward."

"You have a problem with me?"

"Yeah I do. The only reason you are here is because of your father. You are not a pilot. Why don't you go back from where you came from and fly a toy airplane."

"Hey, let me tell you something I have been flying all my life and I have earned the right to fly here."

"Earned? That is a laugh. Who told you that, your father?"

David started to the door. "Excuse me."

"Oh I'll excuse you all right after I'm finished with you." With that Sam pushed David hard sending him back on to the desk. Sam walked to him. "Coward." Sam hit David in his jaw knocking him to the floor.

"Come on coward let's see what you got."

David stood up. "I don't want any trouble with you."

Sam made a fist and drew back to hit David again. David said again. "Don't want any trouble, but if that's the way you want it, okay with me."

David made a fist as Sam swung. David hit him hard sending him back a few steps. "Is that the best you got fly boy?" Sam went to him and kicked his leg knocking David down. David started to stand as Sam hit him in his mouth. Blood ran down his cheek. David wiped the blood as Sam came for more. It was then that David saw what he had to do. He didn't like to fight but now was the time. As Sam got closer David let a hard left fist to Sam's stomach. Sam bent over as David hit him again. Sam again hit David sending him across the desk to the floor. He got up and with a swinging of his foot hit Sam in his mouth. Blood shot from his mouth as he fell to the floor. David ran to him hitting him more and more.

The Captain down the hall heard the noise and came to squad room as David was hitting Sam. "What the hell is going on here?" David backed off and stood. "What is all this fighting about?"

"Ah, nothing sir just a misunderstanding."

"Misunderstanding about what?"

"Well sir, I called him a Frenchie and he called me a Yankee." Sam slowly got to his feet.

The Captain looked at both of them. "I should ground you both but I need you both in the air. Now, both of you shake hands. Fighting is not allowed here. If you want to fight, fight your enemy not each other." David walked to Sam.

"Are you alright?" David extended his hand.

"Yeah, you okay? They shook hands.

"Alright now you two go get cleaned up. You look awful. And don't let this happen again understand."

David and Sam stood at the door. "You're not a coward after all." A smile came to them as they walked down the hall. The Captain looked around the room.

"French and America, God bless us all."

A month passed...It was now...The War...

Sirens rang through the city. Planes call out on the radio. "The enemy is coming...The enemy is coming..." German bombers and fighters were on the way. The war had started. It was late night as the lights of Paris went black.

People ran to shelters and to their homes. The base was on full alert as men scrambled to their quarters waiting for instructions. The night mare was about to happen to Paris, France. Men that were not on the base were called to report immediately to their commander. The ground crews were pushing all aircrafts out on the runways and were ready to be air born. The city and base was on high alert as the enemy planes were heading for Paris. What news on the radios was warning of the assault. Hospitals were scrambling to prepare for the worst. Police were on all the streets getting people to safety.

Chapter 12

Night time can rule your thoughts,
When I was seven years old I was told,
It was the devil's way to make us old,
So I would pray on my knees at night,
Keep us strong and win the fight,
I would go outside at night to show the devil,
I wasn't afraid to fight, that he was wrong,
And I was right,
While mother and dad were in their bed,
I would hold my bible next to my heart,
To show the devil we were strong,
And would not part, I would show no fear,
For I knew, the Lord was near…

The Last Night...

Denise and David stood in the doorway. As their lips parted, their eyes met. A nervous smile and a touch on his cheek, her hands smoothed the collar of his uniform. She touched the star on his chest and the bar on his collar and closed her eyes as his hand ran through her long brown hair. Bombs fell in the distance.

"I must go."

Her fingers traced his lips. "I know."

His strong arms wrapped around her for the last time as he kissed a falling tear from her blue eyes, "But I will be back."

The smell of the uniform told her that he cared. "I know you will."

The planes flew over the buildings. He tilted her chin up to him.

"You are my girl."

She kissed his hand with a faint smile. "Yes, I am, forever."

His hands held her face. "I'll be back, I love you."

He turned and took a step.

"No, wait."

He turned to see her go to a small sewing basket.

She picked up the basket and a smile came as she took a silk scarf and a cap from the basket. "I finished it last night, a silk scarf for your neck and a cap for your hair." She put the scarf around his neck. He took his uniform hat off as she put the cap on his head. She smiled. "Now you are perfect."

He kissed her hands as she adjusted the cap. "I feel perfect."

She took his hand and placed a small tiny silver thimble in his hand.

He held his finger up looking at the thimble. "What is this?"

"It is for luck, so you won't get hurt."

He wiggled his finger with a chuckle and a smile.

"I wore it when I was knitting your cap and scarf."

He kissed it and put it in his jacket pocket. "I'll bring it back to you."

He picked up his bag and walked down the steps. He stopped and blew her a kiss. "Love you."

With that he ran down the street with the scarf trailing behind him. She leaned against the door as tears ran down her face. She whispered.

"Love you."

The time is now...

The French Air Force went into action. American planes and British planes were on their way to help France. Planes left the ground ready for the attack. There were hundreds of planes in the air. The German planes kept coming as the lights shown through the fog of the night. This was it...

David sat in his plane waiting for his orders to fly. The airman waved his arms. All of the squad's planes were lined up and started to roll down the airstrip.

David sat thinking about the last time he and Denise were together. It had been a quite night.

The night air was filled with the smell of flowers Denise had picked and put in a vase. Her smell filled his mind. Her eyes were bright and filled with love.

Love for life, love for the future, love for him. He remembered them sitting on the couch with his arm around her.

He remembered the small little kisses they passed to each other. He remembered putting the envelope behind the pillow.

He remembered the conversation about the house Denise was raised in.

"Honey, it can happen at any time now. Will you go to your house or stay here?"

She cuddled up to him and smiled her wonderful smile. "No more house. I gave it to the church. They will make a hospital there. That is what my mother and father would have wanted. Before they died, they told me to do as I pleased with it. So, I gave it away to help others. I will stay here and wait for you to come to me."

"And I will, I will never leave you never. As soon as I can, I will be back in your arms."

The siren's sound filled his mind and thoughts as he rolled down the runway. He remembered looking back to see her throw a kiss to him.

He remembered standing in the doorway as she put a silk scarf around his neck and a knit hat on his head.

He reached in his jacket pocket and took out a small silver thimble. He kissed it and put it close to his heart. "I love you Denise," he shouted.

Chapter 13

I fell from a tree one time and it was not fun,
I lay there looking up at the sun,
The white clouds seem to wave at me,
My arm hurt but I waved back in my tears,
Wondering if I would die,
That's when I began to cry,
I knew the pain would go away,
And again I would laugh and play,
Then a little bird landed in a tree,
It spoke to me, it is just you and me,
So I got up a little sad, a little mad,
But I was alive and I was glad...

That Night of Fear...

Bombs fell through the night. Planes fell from the sky. Denise stood in the darkness looking out the window. She saw a flash of firing bullets from the planes and people screaming in the night. The smell of death was all around her. Buildings were being bombed. Rockets flew through the air in different directions. The fight was on.

Three bombs bust nearby. The street lit up as if it were daytime. Denise closed her eyes and started to pray. "Dear God, protect him... bring him back to me."

That was the last thing she said before a bomb hit the building she was in. Glass rushed in. Bricks fell. The roof fell in. A large wall pinned her against the window.

Her face bled from the glass. Blood ran fast down her face and pain came to her eyes and head...

She could not see. She could not feel the pain in her side or the broken wood that lay across her neck as she passed out.

Darkness came to her soul. Darkness fell in her mind.

It was a day later that several men dug through the fallen building in search of anyone that might still be alive.

Dogs searched and began to bark at the building she was in. Men rushed to the large wall that had fallen.

It took hours before they reached her. There she lay holding an envelope. Blood had dried on her head and neck. A large scar across her forehead was open. Her dress and shoes were covered with her blood.

As the bricks and wall were removed, two men lifted her limp body and carried her to an ambulance nearby.

A man called out. "Is she dead?"

Another answered. "No but hurry up, don't look good."

It was a crowed hospital. People were badly hurt and some had died. The smell of death filled the room where she lay. Cries and moans of love ones called out. She lay motionless on the bed. Her head was covered with white gauge and tape over her eyes and neck. Her arms and hands were covered with the white material. Blood seeped through the gauge around her head.

Silence filled her mind. The dripping of fluid from the bottle above bed was all that was heard.

A lady doctor and nurse came in to attend her. They examined her and wrote on her chart. The blood has stopped.

"I am a doctor, can you hear me?" Denise did not answer.

"You stay with her and call me when she comes to." The nurse sat on the bed and held Denise's hand.

Six hours had passed. Denise began to stir. Cries of pain came. She called out. "Protect him… Protect him."

The nurse rubbed her arm. "Who honey, who?"

She fell back into a deep sleep. The nurse called for the doctor.

The door opened and the doctor came to Denise's side.

"She said something… "Protect him…protect him."

Two days later, Denise felt the cool sheets of the bed.

The nurse was sitting reading and saw Denise move. She went to her and held her hand.

"It's alright honey, you are safe in a hospital. We are right here with you."

"What happen to me? Why can I not see or feel?"

The nurse called for the doctor. "You will be fine, just relax."

As the doctor came in, Denise cried out. "I can't see."

The doctor sat on the bed and brushed Denise's hair. "I am glad to see you are awake. You slept well. Are you in any pain?"

Denise grabbed her arm. "I can't see."

The doctor looked at the nurse. "I know, and I am sorry, but you are alive and that is good. Your name is Denise Val Jean. We found this letter in your hand. It is a beautiful letter… He must love you very much."

Denise tried to think. She could only remember the lights in the sky and the roar of the night.

"Letter?… My name?…can't think now. My head is not well and my thoughts are not good. Why can I not see?"

"Denise, my child, you were a victim of the war. You were in a building that fell. I am sorry to tell you that."

Denise fell back to sleep.

The next morning the doctor and nurse were changing the bandages on Denise's eye, head and neck. The doctor looked at the nurse. The nurse turned away. There was a large scar on Denise's neck and her eye was not there. The nurse turned to see. "Oh my God."

The doctor continued to dress the eye and neck and head. She put ice on Denise's lips. Denise slowly licks her lips.

"My head is hurting badly. My body is very sore. I am hungry."

The doctor laughed. "Well that is a good sign. Get her something to eat and drink."

The nurse left the room.

"Doctor, why do I have this bandage over my head and eyes?"

The doctor put the towels and water on the stand.

"Denise, I want you to understand this. You are a very lucky girl. There are many that did not make it through what has happen. You did."

The doctor moved close to her. "Now, I must tell you about your eyes and neck. Your neck has been cut very badly. There will be a long scar there, and honey…" She reached for Denise's hand. Denise sensed something was wrong.

"Go on."

"Well honey, you have lost your eye."

Denise heard her but could not believe what she was saying. "I have only one eye? This must not be true." Denise cried out. "Why you say this?"

"Honey, I am so sorry. The broken glass has taken you eye. You are a beautiful girl and I am so sorry. You must go to your friends and they will help you live again. Find the man in your life. Be glad you are alive."

Denise started to cry. "I have no friends, I don't know of David. He knows not of me. How can a one eye person live like this…no David, no friends?"

They are retreating… They are leaving…

The radios echoed. "They are leaving."

David was high in the sky when he heard the news. The pilot beside him gave a thumbs-up. Two German planes were still circling in the sky. David saw them and pointed to Sam the pilot next to him.

"You take that one and I will get this one."

He started his dive from above. His sights were on the German plane. "You're mine feller, you're mine."

His guns started to fire as he got closer to the plane.

The plane was hit and smoke rolled in the sky as it began to fall. It started to spin downward. David let out a yell.

"Got you man, got you."

All of a sudden David's thoughts were of what he had just done. He had killed a man. A man with perhaps a family. A woman that loved this man.

A father of children. David heard the Captain shouting, "Kill before you are killed."

As he watched the plane fall, the second plane came from out of nowhere and opened fire on David's plane. He was hit. Bullets riddled the right side of David's plane. David was hit in his shoulder and side. His arm and leg went dead. He could not feel his side or his leg. The plane started to dive. Smoke filled the cockpit. Pain took over his mind. He struggled to get the seat belt off with his left hand. He heard the Captain calling in his mind. "Bail out David, bail out."

As he pushed the button the canopy opened and he felt the seat belt give way. Air rushed in as the plane went down. The seat flew into the air. His chute opened as he fell to the ocean. He watched the plane explode as it hit the water. He passed out.

British ships were in the waters not far away. They had seen the plane in trouble and had seen the parachute open and David falling. Instantly they went to his aid. The ship circled David's body floating in the waters. British Navy soldiers came to his aid. Hours later he lay in the hospital.

He had lost a lot of blood and lay with tubes feeding him. The cool sheets and hard bed made the room feel as if it were a coffin. David was semi-conscious when the doctors came in. The doctor wrote on the clipboard. He went to David's side and softly shook him.

"Lieutenant Hunt, can you hear me?"

David slowly turned his head to the sound of the doctor. "Water."

The doctor nodded to the nurse. She put ice in his mouth and on his lips. The doctor reached for David's hand and felt his wrist and looked at his watch.

"David, can you talk to me? David, do you know what happen to you?" David opened his eyes slowly looking around him. Everything was burry and out of focus. He started to feel pain and cried out with his pain.

The doctor had the nurse give him a shot for the pain. As she injected the medicine David started to relax. Again the doctor asked.

"David, do you know what happen to you?"

"I can't feel my arm. I can't feel my leg. My head is not there."

"Just relax, let the medicine take affect." The doctor sat on the bed beside him.

"David, you are in a British Hospital. You have been in an accident. Do you remember the accident?"

"No... you call me David, why?"

The doctor looked at the nurse. She handed him the dog tags.

"These are yours. You are an American in the French Air Force. Your plane was shot down, do you remember that?"

"I am what?...I am where?"

The pain hit him again as he cried out holding his shoulder.

"Nurse give him the sleeping medicine, let him rest and sleep. David, I will check back on you every hour. Just rest now."

The doctor and nurse left the room. They stood in the hallway talking.

"Sir, he doesn't look so well."

The doctor started to walk. "I know, he has a long way to go and a rough road to travel."

It was a day later when the doctor and several others came in David's room. David was holding his right shoulder when they came in. His leg was in a cast and high in the air. "Lieutenant Hunt, good morning, these are doctors that assist me in your case." They gathered around the bed. "How do you feel today?"

"Feel?... I can't feel my arm. I can't feel my leg. My body feels like a train hit me. How do you think I feel?"

"David, things are going to be different for you. You have lost your right arm. Your leg has been saved but your foot is badly damaged. I'm sorry son, but it had to be done or you would have died." David started to cry.

He throws his head from side to side. He shouted.

"No, no, why me?"

"David, do you remember your plane? Do you remember being shot down?"

He covered his eyes with his left arm crying. "Why me?"

The doctors started looking at his arm and leg.

"Doctor, this will take a while to heal."

David screamed at them. "Get out…all of you, get out."

The doctor nodded at the others. They left the room.

"David, I will be with you all the way. You will recover. You will walk again. You will live as you have always wanted, but there will be some adjustments that you must make."

David laughed as tears rolled down his face. "Adjustments, no arm, no foot, I can't even remember my name. Oh yeah doctor, there will be adjustments alright."

"David, you are in the best of the hospitals in the world and there are people that will help you recover, and in time, you will be transferred to your country in America, I might add, you are a hero. You shot down an enemy plane. Think about that."

It was several days later as David lay looking at the ceiling. "Hi mate."

David turned to see the man in the bed next to him.

"Name's Ernest, you look much better today."

"Well I don't feel any better."

"Your name is David right? I heard the doc talking about you."

There was a long pause.

"You are American right? I got a lot of American friends. I am an American too." Ernest saw David's pain.

"I lived in California, New York, born in Tennessee. Been here so long I even talk like I'm English."

"Good for you."

"Hey mate, just want to be friends."

David turned back looking at the ceiling. "Got all the friends I need."

"Sorry about your leg and arm mate. Me, I lost my mind, see shot in the head, and I was shot in my leg and my belly. Guess I will be here a while."

"Yeah me to."

"Got family?… me, got some back home."

A tear came as David thought about Denise.

"Guess they will be glad to see you when you get home. Would you like to tell me about you girlfriend?"

David looked to the ceiling and smiled.

"You talked about her in your sleep." David could see her face.

"She is amazing. Candy blue eyes, always with a smile. We met in high school. She is from France. Tall, dark hair, wish I could be with her right now. Funny thing is she gave me a good luck charm. Now look at me."

David called for the nurse. The nurse came and stood by David.

"You called for me sir?"

"Yes, could you bring me my flight jacket?"

"Sure, I'll get it right now."

David again looked to the ceiling.

Shortly the nurse came back with the jacket. "Is this what you are looking for?" She laid the jacket on the bed and went away.

David searched the jacket. "Aww, here it is. Take a look at this. She gave it to me before I went to war."

David kissed the tiny silver thimble and throws it over to Ernest. He looked it over. "What the hell is this?"

David chuckled. "You never have seen a thimble? You wear it so you don't stick yourself when you are sewing. It protects you. It protects you..." David thought about her last words, "This will protect you and bring you back to me."

Ernest throws it back to David. "Well it did. You are still alive and you will see her again."

David held it to his heart and closed his eyes.

David's thoughts of Denise and their apartment came to him. He felt her putting the silk scarf around him neck. He felt her kiss and saw her waving as he ran down the street. "I hope so."

A nurse came in the ward calling to the men. "Mail call." Days went by as David hoped to get mail from Denise but nothing ever came. Months passed. All of David's letters came back to him saying, "Return to Sender." Denise was lost.

He had nothing to live for. Every night he cried to God to find her, to bring them together again.

A year had passed and he was ready to go back to America. Home was never the same. His mother and father had died and so had Denise.

The Inter-War was over...1938

The Germans had retreated and had lost the war and it was over.

The destruction they had left was one that was one for the history books. France did declare war on Germany and was victorious September 3, 1939 and the Germans had got what they had deserved.

The war was over...but putting the pieces back would take a long time. No one ever knew why the Germans retreated, why they came in the first place.

The short destruction of the city and the many people that were removed from their homes were an unknown mystery. Even the history books cannot say for sure why it happened. One thing is for sure; the love for the city of Paris was strong and would prevail.

Chapter 14

Never give up is what my dad taught me,
Always have hope and faith in yourself,
I have always heard him saying that,
Even when I failed at something,
His words were there for me,
Love is like that, you can't give up,
Even the darkness of night has a way,
To give you the strength to search your
Heart and find what is important to us.
Today, I have found the light and know
That I will prevail no matter what...
I will never give up.

Alone at Home

David wandered the American streets for two years always thinking of what might have been with Denise. The plans that they had made, the love that they had shared, the dreams of the future, the everlasting thought of her smiling face and soft touch would never be again.

Yes, letters were lost between Denise and David. For years there was no contact between them. The streets of America were an empty place.

He looked at the cane in his hand and would think of the boy that ran down the street with a scarf around his neck and a funny hat on his head. He felt his arm and remembered the soft touch of her body as he held her. Never again would that happen again.

Denise was found under the fallen building and was put in the hospital where she lost her eye and a scar on her neck. For many years she tried to recover from the scars that filled her mind. The thought of David was only a passing thought. A passing thought of love. She knew she would never know what happened to him. When released from the hospital she wandered in the city of Paris. No friends, no job or money, no home....

David lost his arm and his foot was damaged badly. He stayed in the British Hospital for almost a year. Many letters were written to Denise only to be returned. He went back to America to find that his mother and father had died in an automobile accident.

His stay in the American hospital was long and so was the rehabilitation of his arm and leg. After more than a year, his thoughts of being alone drew him back to the streets of Paris France. He longed for Denise and went back to Paris hoping to find her. From time to time he would walk the city streets in hopes that someone knew of her but no one knew of her.

Always Hope for Love...

It was a foggy night as David walked the streets of Paris France that he wandered along the pier of the water's edge. With cane in hand he tapped the pier's hard ground.

As he slowly walked, he saw in the dim light and a figure sitting in the shadows of the street light. As he approached the woman she held out her hand. "A penny, a nickel." The tapping of the cane stopped in the night.

"Ain't got much." He took out all the change from his pocket. "Looks like about sixteen cents." He put it in her hands. Again he fished in his pocket. Thought I had more change. He felt his pocket again.

"Oh, I got this old thimble, you can have it..., and its good luck you know." He put it in her hand. "It was for me." He smiled and walked away.

She dropped the change and held the thimble to the light looking at it as the tapping of the cane went away into the dark of the night.

Tears came to her as she held the tiny thimble. She looked into the darkness.

Bombs, fire, smoke, exploded in her mind. She kissed the tiny silver thimble as thoughts of a young man ran down the street with a scarf and cap. She started to cry as she looked into the gray fog…

"David, was that you?"

The tapping came back and stopped as he stood looking at her.

"Denise, is that you?" She smiled and nodded her head.

He slowly sat beside her. "Denise, I said I would be back to you. Do you remember that little thimble?… It brought me back."

"Yes David I remember everything, and I still love you very much." The war had not erased what they had.

"I haven't got an arm or a good leg, but I still have that thimble you gave me, and I love you more today than ever."

She smiled and leaned to him. "A little kiss for an old one eyed lady." He leaned and kissed her.

He took the thimble and put it on her finger.

"Denise, will you still marry me? We can go to America and have a great life together. I have a big house and lots of money."

She just laughed. "You silly old man, all I want is to be with you, always."

She took the thimble and put it on his finger... "Will you still marry me?"

"You know I will. And do you remember that promise you made me long ago. You said you would read the poem you wrote for me."

Denise searched her mind. "My book was lost in the war but I will say the words to you, someday." She laughed. "Someday."

David laughed too. "You always say that, someday."

A happy, The End...

Cory sat waiting to hear more. "Did they go back to America? Did they get married? Do they have any kids?"

His uncle laughed. "That is a good question. We kind of lost contact. War is just that way. The last letter I got from him, he said that they were very happy in America and they were doing fine."

"What happened to the thimble?"

Ernest shook his head. "It's funny about that, how something like a small silver sewing thimble can hold love forever. But it did for them. Funny ain't it how loving does things. I will never forget the look in his face as he told me about her. She must be some kind of lady. I know that he was a very special kind of man."

Cory stood and picked up some of the wood his uncle had cut. "Thanks for telling me that story. Now

I know what love means. Even the little things that we love can make a difference. I'll be glad when I fall in love." "Oh you will someday. People do hold on to all kinds of love things. My last wife, God bless her soul, she put a flower I gave her in her old bible that was our love for each other. Every time I open that old bible I think about her smiling at me."

"Wow that is a great story to tell."

"Yep but not like the story of David and Denise, That's a special story."

Conclusion

It was early morning as the large ship entered the harbor of New York. "David look"

"Yes the Statue of Liberty, a gift from France to all America. This is called Liberty Island. She has been here over a hundred years in the New York harbor. It represents freedom and democracy. Do you know the Frenchman who created her?"

"Yes, I studied French history in school. His name was Auguste Barthoidi."

"Yes it was. Isn't she beautiful?"

It was a great ride home in the cab as Denise marveled at the tall buildings along the way. As the cab pulled up to the house, Denise looked at David. "Is this your house?"

"No, it's our house."

She looked at the large front yard and the large house. "It is so big. Do you cut the grass?"

"No silly, I have a gardener and a man that helps me with things. Oh, wait till you meet Mildred. She is the housekeeper. She wants to meet you very badly. She will do all the things you would like her to do for you."

"You mean a maid?

"Well kind of. I think of her as family."

As they walked up the stairs to the door, it opened and there stood Mildred.

"Oh Mr. Hunt it is so glad you returned safely. And you must be Mrs. Hunt." Mildred went to Denise with a big hug.

"I am pleased to meet you Mildred and please call me Denise."

"Yes ma'am. Denise. Please come in. Can I get you anything? The trip must have tired you both, and your room is ready for you. I will get you some tea and serve it to you in the living room."

It was late evening as they sit watching the glow of the fire burning in the large fireplace.

"This is a wonderful house. Mildred is a very kind person."

"Yes she is and will do anything for you. Would you like to see my mother and dad a long time ago?"

"Yes that would be nice. You have talked about them and it would be fitting to see them again."

David went to the bookcase and got the photo album. "Okay, this is my life." David opened the album and laughed.

"This is my mother and me on a picnic. She was an amazing woman. This is my father and me standing by the first plane that I flew. He taught me everything about flying. This is my favorite picture, my dog and buddy, Loaner."

"Loaner? That is a funny name for a dog."

David laughed. "The story is that a girl gave him to me and I didn't know if I could keep him so she said, 'Just call him Loaner,' and I did. I kept him in the barn till about a week later my father came in the barn and saw me feeding him. He said, "Why don't you bring him in the house? He is going to be a big dog." So I did. He grew to be a big dog. A very big German Shepard. Let me tell you a story about him. My mother and dad went on a trip out of state, and I stayed with my grandmother while they were gone. One night Loaner started barking and scratching at the door so I let him out. He started running to my house. There was two men robbing the house and Loaner ran in and attacked the men. A man shot him in his leg and ran away. They set off the alarm and the police came. When they came in, they saw Loaner standing over a man growling. He had saved the house."

"Amazing, what happen to him?"

"Well he had a bad limp, and dad thought he would be better off if he could help others so he went to a place to be trained to help a blind person and he did, a little girl."

"Did you ever see him again?"

"No but I'm sure he is still helping that little girl." David kept looking at the picture of Loaner. Denise saw his feeling for Loaner.

"I love dogs why don't we get one. We could call him Loaner 2. That would make me very happy, us happy."

David looked at her smiling face. "That would be great."

"Would you like to take a walk down by the pond?"

"Is there tall grass where we can make love?"

"Make love? Wow it has been so long I forgot how."

"Me too, but they say you never forget." And they did.

Wish I could…

The next day they were sitting on the front porch, David in the swing and Denise rocking in her rocking chair. A small boy about the age of ten came up to the porch.

"Hi, are you Mr. Hunt? Here is your paper."

"Yes I am and thank you very much."

"Wow, someday when I grow up I want to be just like you.

A real hero with a big house, and a beautiful wife. I want to learn to fly an airplane just like you sir."

David smiled and laughed. "Tell you what young man, I have a model plane in the house that needs to be put together maybe you can help me. That's how I got started."

"That would be great sir I'll be back tomorrow."

Denise sat rocking and watching them talk. She thought back into the past to see a young boy in uniform running down the street with a scarf around his neck and a funny hat on his head. She could hear the words, "I love you and I'll be back." She remembered sewing the scarf and the tiny silver, "Thimble."

A gift she will always treasure.

This story is true, some things were changed.

As a young boy in Tennessee, my uncle told me this story. No, he was not David, but he was a pilot and a friend of that man. Although this story is fiction, some parts are true. This story has also been created by the author's imagination.

Romance and Love comes in many different colors.
Romance is a feeling. Romance can find you anywhere.
As you can find Romance anywhere.
Love is also a feeling. There is a difference.
Romance comes from your mind...
While Love, comes from your heart...
Romance can be lost when parted from each other.
While Love, can never be separated if you are apart.

"Thimble"
Continues...

A Poem from Denise

My thoughts wandered in darkness until I met him.
The days went by slowly and the nights flew,
My heart felt empty like the darkness of the blue,
Then a bright light shined down
and I knew it was you.
So tall and handsome when you held me tight,
I knew in my heart everything would be alright.
The touch of his lips, his eyes so
blue, a love I knew was true,
Always and forever he whispered to me,
Again my heart felt as deep as the sea.
I will give him a child, I will give all my love,
He brightens my life like the heavens above.
The angels sing when I look in his face,
My darkness has passed away from me,
I have found love now and I can see at last.
The kiss we share, holding hands as we walk,
Can only add to the joy in my heart,
And I know our love will never part.
I will breathe his name as death I do part,
Till we meet in heaven and again we will start.

David, I will always love you, you
have gave me eyes so I can
see our future. You have given me
hope again. You have given
of yourself to me and to France.
You are my hero.
Love always,
Denise

PART 2

"THIMBLE"

Months had gone by as Denise and David were as happy as could be.

It was a warm light as they had just finished their dinner. Denise was putting dishes away and David was resting in his favorite chair reading. She came into the living room and sat looking at the blank television set. David put his book down and saw Denise staring at the television.

"You want me to turn it on?"

Denise just sat quite.

"Sweetheart, is something wrong?"

She came to him and sat at his feet. "Nothing is wrong, it's just I have been thinking about being here in America. People help each other here more that in France. I mean they do there to but I see on television that people help people. David I want to help America as you have help France."

David laughed. "You want to fly a plane?"

Denise hit his leg. "No silly but I feel that I could help women here in some way."

"What do you have in mind?"

"I don't know yet." She looked up at him. "David do you look at me in a different way now that I have only one eye? Do you see this black patch?"

"Stop right there. What I see is a beautiful woman. There is no patch. Let me ask you something. When you look at me, do you see a one arm man?"

"I see a brave man. A man I love very much. When you hold me in your arm it is like walking in heaven. I can feel your heart beating and the love you have for me. Your one arm is all I need."

David smiled. "You always say the words I long to hear. Let me think about what you have said. There could be an answer."

"What do you mean an answer?"

David sat back in his chair thinking and looking at her.

"If I have learned anything, there is an answer to all questions."

Let's go somewhere...

Another week had passed as David hung up the phone. David sat thinking about the phone call he had just made. Yes there was an answer to all questions. Just one more question had to be answered and that was when and where to tell Denise.

The morning was a beautiful one as David came into the kitchen where Denise was. He put his arm around her and held her tight.

"What are you doing?"

"Making breakfast for us. How you like eggs? Easy or scrambled?"

"Today, scrambled."

She laughed. "Good that's the way they turned out."

David laughed. "Say, how would you like to take a trip somewhere?"

"I would love that. It has been long time since we have been some place."

"Great. I know a place you would love to see. It is high in the mountains where the air is as clean and as pure as in heaven and you can almost touch the clouds in the sky."

"That sounds wonderful."

"Okay I'll make plans to go there. You will love it there. You can buy stuff and we can make love all week."

"Buy stuff? What does that mean? Buy stuff?"

David laughed. "Anything you want. And we can dance, and eat and just relax. The world is yours sweetheart, anything you want."

Denise kissed him. "You wash up and your scrambled eggs will be ready for you… Anything?"

David hugged her tightly with a kiss. "Anything you want."

David made the plans for the trip. That day they went shopping for their needs. Denise was very excited about going away. At lunch Denise turned to David. "What about Loaner 2? Where will he stay? Or go with us maybe."

David took a pad from his pocket jacket. "I have taken care of that. He will stay at a very good shelter called "Pets best friend." They will take very good care of him."

"Good. You know he is really getting big and very smart. The other day he went to the mail box and brought mail back to me."

"Yes and he has learned to protect you to. All you have to say to him is, "Protect me" and he will."

Denise took a bite. "Will he protect me from you?"

David laughed. "Well he's my friend to you know. Are you ready for desert?"

"What did you have in mind? Love making?"

"Later, for sure but for now how about chocolate mousse?"

"Yes, both." She giggled as a small girl would.

It was a night of passion as they lay in bed. Denise got up and went to the bay window looking out at the silver moon and all the stars. She turned to him watching him sleep. A star tinkled as she looked back out the window. She looked into the darkness. "Thank you Lord for all you have given to me. I am not worthy for such a kind loving man as he is. He has given me so much hope. I only pray that you will allow me to give him as much as he gives. Let us always be a part of your world and protect him from any harm. I ask this in your name, amen."

A warm glow went through her body as if her prayer had been heard. She turned looking at David. She knew that all would be alright now.

Loaner stood barking at the front door. Denise went to see what he was barking at. A truck had stopped and a man with a package was coming. She opened the door as he knocked. "It's alright Loaner."

"Good morning mam, package for Mrs. Hunt."

"That is me."

"Just sign here Mrs. Hunt."

She took the package and signed the paper.

"Thank you mam and have a good day." With that he left the house.

She hurried to the living room to open the package. When she opened it her mouth opened wide. It was a diamond bracelet and matching ear rings with a note inside.

"You are my every breath, my every heartbeat, my all. David"

She started to cry. She ran through the house calling his name. David had left the house but left a note on the pillow.

"Will be back soon, love you." She hugged the note. "Love you to my husband."

It was later when David came into the house. She ran to him and hit his behind. "Why did you not tell me you were leaving? I was worried about you. Don't leave me again not telling me."

"I'm sorry honey but it was important that I had to go out. Didn't you get my call?"

"I don't know how to answer that machine,"

David laughed. "Well, I'll teach you. Come on, I'll show you again."

They went into his office. "Okay, first you press this button then." She stopped him. "Not now, it is too hard to learn. Machines are not my best thing to learn. Even the cell phone is hard to understand."

"Okay sweetheart, I will show you some other time."

"Merci for understanding, dinner is almost ready. You will like what I fixed."

"I'm sure I will. Let's go eat."

And it was everything he liked. Fried chicken, mashed potatoes, corn bread, ice tea, and fudge brown cake.

David pushed away from the table. "My am I full, how did you learn to cook this good?"

She smiled. "Oh it is easy. You just call the chicken place and tell them what you want."

David laughed out loud and went to her with a kiss. "Damn you're smart."

A book would be nice...

It was late evening. Loaner lay asleep beside David and Denise. The news was on the television. Denise reached for the remote control and turned it off. "Can we talk? There is something we can talk about. I have been thinking about helping people."

"Sure honey, tell me all about it."

"Well I watch the television and have learned that there are lots of women that I can help."

"Oh yeah, how?"

"The war I will never forget. There are others that have been in a war to. Maybe not even been in a war that has lost an eye, an arm, and their beauty. How do they feel? So, I ask myself, how can I help them as I have lost my eye and have a very long scar on my neck and lost my beauty?"

"Wait a minute."

"No hear me out. I thought maybe I could write a book telling them they are not alone, that there is hope for them, that they are not the only one that might have this problem. I just want to help others someway."

"I never thought you felt this way. I think you are right but as I have said to you many times, the lost of your eye does not mean that you are not beautiful to me." He kissed her and went on talking.

"I would love you if you were blind but I see your point and I will help you with your book or anything you want to do. What can I do to make you happy?"

"I don't know David. You know a lot of people and maybe they have an answer for me."

"Okay sweet, I do know a writer friend of mine and I will call her and set an appointment for you to meet and tell her what you have in mind for your book." Denise smiled and hugged him.

"I knew you would have the answer for me. I will repay you later in bed. Is that alright with you?"

David picked her up and started up stairs. "Later? What about now? I even have another answer for you and I will tell you about it next week."

"Next week? No David you tell me now. Is it another gift I can wear?"

"Kinda, we will see. I think you will like it better than diamonds."

The day started off on a bright sunny morning as Denise ran down the stairs to open the door. A well-dressed lady stood there with a brief case in one hand and a notebook in the other. "Hi, are you Denise?"

"Yes I am. Can I help you?"

"I am Charlotte Watts, and your husband has told me all about you. I am a writer. He said that you are interested in writing a book."

"Oh yes, please come in to our house. I was not expecting you so soon."

"My, what a beautiful house you have here. I just love these older big houses. I guess I should have called to let you know I was coming."

"Not to worry I love surprises. David does that all the time to me. Tea?"

"That would be lovely."

"Please sit and I will have Mildred bring us something."

They sat talking about France and how Denise met David.

Charlotte got her note pad out and started to write. "This is going to make a great story and such a happy ending."

"I suppose but that is not the story I am talking about."

"Oh, what did you have in mind?" Denise told her about helping other women. At the end Charlotte was amazed and kept writing and turning pages.

"Denise, I know I can help you and I will also help you get a manager to see your book through. Publishing is a very hard way to go. I can also see you on television telling your story to women you want to reach."

Denise put her hand over her eye and neck. She remembered the wall falling and the cry for help coming from the streets outside the apartment.

"No television please, just a book."

"But look at the millions of viewers you could talk to in just a minute. A book will take some time to publish and get to an audience of women that you want to read about. Television is the right way."

"Maybe, but I am not ready for to be seen. I hope you will understand."

Charlotte closed the note pad. "I think I do honey, I think I do." Charlotte stood. "Tell you what, I'll go and put things down on paper and let you see if you like the way I write about your experiences. Then we will take it from there. I'm sure there are things you did not tell me about, well you know."

"Merci for your time and understanding. Yes, I know and I have forgotten most things thanks to David."

"Yes he is an amazing man. Denise I also think you are an amazing woman and it has been a pleasure to have met such a woman such as yourself."

"Merci and thank you for your kind words. David was right about you, you are a true friend. It has also been a pleasure to have met you."

"I'll be in touch soon. Bye for now Denise."

Are you ready?

David entered the house with his cane and a limp. Slowly he went and sat down. Denise was standing in the living room and saw him in pain. She went to him. "David, what happen to you? Why are you limping like that? Are you alright?"

"Oh it's nothing. Just fell down a few stairs. Nothing to worry about."

"Let me see. You have torn your pants. This is your sore leg too."

"Yes it is but I'll be okay. Would you fix me a good strong drink?"

Denise went to the cabinet and got him a glass of scotch. She looked at him as he put his leg up on the couch. She went to him and sat down at his feet.

"Maybe you should see the doctor. I will call him and he will come."

"We will see, maybe later if it still hurts me." He opened his brief case and took out a map and a brochure. "Look at this. It is where we will be staying. It will take us along the coastline so you can see just how beautiful the trip will be. It will take about eight hours to get there but we can stop along the way to have lunch and shop if you want to."

"My, the hotel is very big. Look David, the room has a spa in it and a king size bed and a wet bar. Look at the view we will have." David watched her face as she look at the pamphlet. She was more radiant than she ever was. His thoughts were of a French girl long ago full of love, excitement, smiles, and a glow about her he would never forget. She had had a rough life and he wanted to try to make up for that. "So my beautiful wife, when would you like to go? If we leave on Thursday night we will be there on Friday about noon. What do you say?"

"I say merci my favorite husband. Oh David this is so nice of you. I can not wait till we are dancing under the stars. Just you and I."

"That is all I ever wanted is just you and I to be together."

She kissed his leg. "I am so sorry about your leg. I will care for you anyway you want."

The evening was quiet as they sat watching a movie on television.

David sat with his leg propped up and Denise looking over the pamphlet.

"It says here that breakfast can be served in the room. Is that true?"

"Oh yeah and lunch to but we have so much to do that we will have lunch at a nice restaurant away from the hotel. Did you see the sky lift they have? It will take us all the way to the top of the mountain. There you can touch the sky and the clouds."

"That is what I want to do is hold hands and touch the heavens."

David smiled and laughed. "Then that is what we will do."

"Have I told you that I amour you more than yesterday?"

"Not today but merci tre's beaucoup."

"Vous etes l'accueil. Oh, let me tell you something. Your friend Charlotte, the writer, came by and we had a very good talk. She is very nice and will help me with the book. She took notes and said she would put things on paper for me to see and approve if I like the things she wrote."

"That is good news."

"And she said something about being on television to talk to other women, but I don't think I want to do that."

"Might not be a bad idea. You can reach a lot of women that way and fast." Denise touched the long scar on her neck and held her hand over the patch.

"That may be true but I am not comfortable with that."

"Well one step at a time sweetheart, one step at a time."

"It is late and you should get rest for your leg. Can I help you to come to bed?"

"No, you go on up, I'll be up in a while I have a few things to do with some reports that I should turn in to the office tomorrow."

"Do not be too long my husband. I love saying that."

"Bonne nuit a vous."

"You speak French good for an American." She laughed and giggled.

"Good night to you to."

To the mountains we go...

It was Thursday morning. Denise shook David.

"Wake up sleepy head. You know what day this is." David stretched and sat up. He looked at the clock and lay back down.

"You had better get up. Breakfast ready and it is getting cold. You don't want cold eggs do you?"

Again David sat up as she gave him his robe. She bounced down the stairs like a little school girl. She put the newspaper on his plate and sat down. David appeared at the kitchen door with his cane.

"What's the rush to have breakfast?" He sat down and took a sip of his coffee.

"It's Thursday. Do you not forget what we do today?"

"Thursday, oh yeah. We play cards with the Wilsons right?"

"No silly man, we go to the mountains and the beautiful hotel."

He smiled. "Just kidding with you, I know. Have you packed with your things?"

"Yes I packed all things and for you to. I am a smart girl you know."

"And a very special girl to. Guess we should leave about noon." She looked at her watch. "It is ten o four now. Is the car ready?" She drank her milk and went around the table to him and sat on his lap. "I love you." She kissed his head and ran to the kitchen door and turned to him.

"We have time to fool around if you want. A quickie?"

He looked at her. "Where did you hear that word quickie?"

"I read it in this magazine Charlotte gave me. What is quickie? It says here that women like a quickie."

David scratched his head. "Ah, I'll explain it to you later. Oh, and don't take that magazine with us."

"But it tells me things I need to know." She held the magazine for him to see.

"See the title of the magazine is WOMEN SPEAK OUT and it says that love making can be done anywhere. Can we do a quickie?"

"You are ready aren't you? Maybe in the car."

"No car, in bed." She patted her butt and smiled. "Come."

Romance is the key, Love is the answer...

"Are you ready Denise? Hurry we have to drop off Loaner at the dog home."

Denise carried two bags into the room and set them by the door. "Wow, they weight a lot. Maybe I pack too much."

He put down his cane and picked one up. "Maybe you did. I'll go unlock the trunk."

She again picked them up and waddled out to the car. "I hope someone will help me with these bags when we get there."

"I'm sure they will. Ready?"

It was a great ride for Denise as she pointed out everything she saw. She kept looking at all the signs that said miles to the mountains. David would laugh at her every time she said, "Not too much miles there." She was the most loving and a wonder to be around. Even the words that she would mispronounce made her even more special to him.

It was two hours into the ride that David looked over to see her sleeping. Ahead was a rest area with a small café they could get something to eat and rest for a while. David pulled into the parking lot and stopped. As soon as he did Denise sat up and yawned.

"Are we here yet? This do not look like the brochure." David laughed.

"No sweetheart this is the halfway point. Want some lunch? Sign says that "WE HAVE THE BEST HAMBUGERS.""

"And some of the French fries too. I'm French you know." She smiled at him.

"Okay French lady, fries it is."

As they entered the café a lady came to them. "Welcome, table for two?"

"Yes please by a window."

Denise looked around. "Why she asked table for two. There is no other with us. I do not understand."

David took her hand and followed the lady to the table by the window. "Because, well I really don't know."

Denise sat looking at the room and a fish mounted on the wall.

"Look, a big fish. That is what I will have a big fish."

"You're right me too."

The lady came to the table. "Are you ready to order?"

"Yes we are. Two orders of that big fish plate with everything and tea."

"Coming right up sir."

Denise looking around saw the music box. "Can I play the machine? I love music while eating."

David fished in his pocket and gave her two quarters. "Here you go." He watched her make her way to the machine. As she walked she bumped into a man at a table. A glass turned over on the table. "Hey look where you're going."

David stood with him cane and went to the man. "What did you say to my wife?"

"She spilled most of my water."

"Like this." David took the glass and threw the rest of the water in his face. "You're a very rude person mister. Now do you want to apology to her?" David hit the table with his cane. The man looked at Denise.

"I'm very sorry. Forgive me?" Denise looked at David then to the man.

"I do kind sir, I do." The man left the café and they went back to their table.

"You did not have to do that David. It was I that made a mistake."

"No it wasn't. He was just a loud mouth and I had to do something."

The fish and chips were very filling as they got into the car and started off on their trip. Denise pushed the button and the window went down. She put her hand out and made waves as the wind passed over her hand.

"Thank you."

"For what?"

"Back there. It was very nice to know that you love and protect me."

"You are worth it and you are right, I do love you very much."

Denise saw a sign. "Look, only one hundred and twenty more miles till there."

"Yep so sit back listen to some music and take a nap."

"Not sleepy and do not want to miss anything along the way. This country is so beautiful. The hills remind me of France."

"You miss France don't you but you never say you do. Why?"

"I guess it was the war. I thought I would never see you again."

He patted her leg and smiled. "Remember that tiny sliver thimble you gave me and I told you that I would be back, remember?"

"Yes, I will always remember that and you did too."

"Well, I will always be by your side and help you and protect you always."

"I am so sorry about your arm and leg. I think sometimes that it was my fault you were hurt fighting for France and for me."

"Sweetheart it was worth everything I went through and you were the prize in the end. Yep, I have no arm or foot but I have you."

Now for great news.

The long ride had ended as they pulled up in front of the grand hotel. An attendant came running to the car and opened the door for David. He then ran around the car and opened the door for Denise. David threw him the keys. "Could you have it washed and gassed up for me please?" David with cane walked to Denise who was standing looking at the tall building.

"This is marvelous. I have never see such a hotel before. Can we quick go in?"

As they entered the hotel the manager quickly came to them.

"You must be Mr. and Mrs. Hunt. We have been expecting you and everything is ready for you. Mr. Hunt it is a pleasure to have you and Mrs. Hunt with us. May I show you around the hotel?"

"No thank you, maybe later. It was a long drive." Denise stood looking at the tall ceiling with the artwork painted high above.

"Look, I know the Frenchman who first painted that drawing. And look David at the chandelier with all though lights. I love it here David."

"Me too sweet. Can you have our bags brought to our room?"

"Right away sir. Mr. Hunt I have read about you and it is an honor to have met such an American hero and for you to stay with us here."

"Thank you but that was long ago. The real hero is my wife Denise Val Jean. If it weren't for her, I would not be here."

Mrs. Hunt if you desire anything, please, ask for me. I am at your service."

"Merci, I may do that."

The rooms were as expected, large, beautiful, and very rich looking. Denise floated around the room and ran to the patio that looked out over the ocean. "Heaven that is all I can say to you Mr. Hunt. You have brought me to heaven. Come see this view." He came to her side looking out at everything.

"Yes it is and I have an angel right here on earth." The kiss was only one that they had for each other. As they looked at each other they knew it too.

David went and sat in a big recliner and put his feet up.

Denise came to him. "Does your leg hurt you? I will get your medicine for you."

"No I'm fine just a little tired. Let me rest a while then we will go shopping. Would you like that? They have plenty of things I know you would like."

"No shopping now, later. Maybe we take a walk on the land by the water."

"Just what I was thinking of, I love you Denise."

"I love everything about you Mr. David Hunt.

It was the third day at the hotel. David stood looking out at the water and the waves washing on to the shore. He was thinking about how to tell Denise the news that the doctor and he had talked about. The news that would change her life. Holding on the rail he paced back and forth. Tonight would be the right time. It was tonight or never.

Denise came in caring two large bags and in her singsong voice she sung out. "David, where are you?" She put the bags down and went out on the patio where he was. "You no hear me? I say, David where are you."

"Hi baby, you are back early. What did you get?"

"Wait till you see what I found for you. I got you something for your desk and something for you to wear."

"Well let's go have a look."

Quickly she went to the table and opened the bag. She brought out a pen, paper, and a blotter for his desk. "You like?"

"Very much, just what I needed for my desk."

"Oh wait till you see this. I know you will be pretty in this." She pulled out a long white robe and handed it to him. She stood back as he tried it on.

"Oh yes, very pretty on you."

He turned around showing it off to her. "You got me exactly what I have always wanted. How did you know?"

"I see you walk in your shorts in the morning walking around the house so I look for you to wear this with my love. I am glad you like it."

"I love it, thank you very much and white is my color to." He went to her with a big hug. "What would I ever do without you? What did you buy for yourself?"

"Oh many things, and something special for tonight."

"Speaking of tonight, we have reservations for us out on the hotel porch under the stars. A romantic table for just us, and that is not all, dancing with the band playing our song."

"A romantic evening, oh I dream of such a night with you."

"Now would you like to take that walk on the land by the water?"

She walked to him and grabbed his hand. She led him to the bedroom door. "Not now. There are more important things to do if you are not too tired."

They walked to the bedside and she pushed him down on it. He smiled.

"Lady, I am never too tired to make love to you." She giggled and jumped on him. She unbuttoned his shirt and unzipped his pants.

"Make love to me all day. Something I thought of all day today."

Now or never...

The restaurant was very busy with people enjoying the food and music. As they entered the large dining room the manager came to them.

"Good evening Mr. and Mrs. Hunt. My you look elegant Mrs. Hunt. Sir, everything is prepared for you to enjoy your meal tonight. Please follow me to your outside romantic table. The night is ready for a romantic night for two people in love. Please enjoy the food and the night and the music."

The soft music drifted out from the room. The sound of the water hitting the lands shore. The candle light flicking, the sound of laughter coming from the people having fun. David looked across the table and reached for Denise's hand.

"You are the most beautiful lady I have ever seen."

Denise brushed her hair back showing the earrings and raised her hand showing the diamond bracelet she wore. "I feel beautiful for the first time in a long while."

David kissed her hand. "I am very happy to have you as my wife."

"This is a wonderful time we have now being together like this."

"It is and I feel this may be the start of an even more beautiful life for you."

David stood. "Would you give me the pleasure of a dance my wife?"

She stood and bowed to him. "It would be my honor sir." The moon cast a glow around them as they held each other. They laughed and kissed as never before. David's heart beat fast as he thought about what he wanted to say to her. Something that would be a turning point in their lives. He had thought what he would say to her and hope it would turn out all right.

With their love so strong he knew that he was doing the right thing for them both. As he held her in him arm and her arms around him he felt secure in what he was about to do. They kissed deeply as the music stopped. It was now or never. They sat down and he reached for her hand.

"Denise there is something I would like to talk to you about. I hope you will not take it the wrong way. I went to see a doctor last week." A well-dressed man came to their table. He handed them a menu and asked. "When you are ready to order sir, I will be your waiter. My name is Jon."

"Thank you Jon we will call you when we are ready."

Denise looked at David. "You saw a doctor? Are you all right? Is it your leg and foot? David you scare me. What is wrong with you?"

"It is not me sweetheart, it is you that we talked about."

"Me? I am not sick I feel wonderful."

"I know that. It is about you're..." David had come to that point he hated.

"It is about your eye."

"My eye? What are you saying to me?"

"His name is Doctor Bain. He is an ophthalmologist. He can do a corneal transplant on your eye so you can see again. He has a staff of doctors and their success is very high in this field. He has done hundreds of this type of transplants. I know this is sudden to talk to you about, but I would love for you just to see him and talk to him. I have talked to several people that he has given their sight back to them, and they all say that it is a wonderful life to be able to see again."

"David are you ashamed of me with my one eye and this patch?"

"Of course not, just hear me out, you will be able to see again. I love you even if you don't want to do this. I see you try to hide that patch, and I know it is hard for you sometimes as you meet people but think about it, you will see again."

"I do not know what to say. I have had the blind eye for many years. I must think of this. It is all new for me to think about."

"Let me tell you about all this. You will have a new eye the same as you had before. The same color, the same sight, everything as you looked before. Your new eye has been given to you by a girl the same age as you are now. It is a perfect match. It only takes less than two months, and you will see again and have perfect vision no scars. See again the rest of your life, would that make you happy to see again without the patch."

Denise sat very quiet. Many things went through her mind. The war, the bombs falling, the fires and smoke. The building falling on her, the hospital. The pain she went through.

"Excuse me David." She got up and walked away from the table.

David sat holding his head with his hand. He kept thinking had he done the right thing. Had he pushed her away from him forever? Maybe he had done the wrong thing in trying to help her this way. He sat there for almost an hour, thinking about what he had said and done. She came back and sat down. She had been crying, and he saw this.

"Forget everything I have said. I am very sorry to have brought this up to you, but I thought you may want to see again and did not know how to tell me about your feelings. I'm sorry honey."

She reached for his hand and kissed it. She looked straight into his eyes and smiled.

"Tell me more. Will I be able to thank the girl for this gift?"

David thought about his answer to that question. He did not want to alarm her.

"There is a policy that the donor will not see or talk to the one that gets the eye. It is a gift from her to you and no words of thanks to be offered."

"I understand and I will accept the eye. Thank you David."

David stood up and shouted. "This is my wife." He ran around the table and kissed her over and over forgetting about his foot.

"Sweetheart I will be with you all the way. You have made me very happy and I will treasure you always." He shouted again to the heaven.

"This is my wife and she will see again. Thank you God, thank you for her."

They lay quite in bed that night. David was staring at the ceiling. Denise looking out the window in thought.

"Will there be pain?"

He reached for her hand and held it tight. "You have known pain, this will not pain as you have known. I am so proud of you for doing this. For you to see again as you did long ago. Remember that young man running down the street with that funny hat and long scarf, well I do and I remember your candy blue eyes and you standing in the doorway waving at me. Well I am about to see your eyes again soon."

"Will you see me differently without the patch on my eye?"

"Yes I will. I will see the girl in you and the woman that I married."

"I never thought this would happen. I never thought I would see again." She rolled over and kissed him. "You have made this all possible. You really do love me don't you?"

David kissed her. "You are my every breath and you always will be."

"But what about you, you do everything for me. I want to help you."

"You fulfill everything in my life. I may not get an arm, and I can walk just fine with my cane, what more can I ask for. I am a very happy man."

Going home, things to do...

The week went very fast and had come to an end. They had done everything they wanted to do and now it was time to go home. It seemed that the trip going home was shorter that getting there. As they pulled up to their house Mildred came running to meet them.

"Mr. Hunt, Mrs. Hunt, it is so good to have you back safe. I have food for you and the house is glad you are home too."

"We had a wonderful trip Mildred and it is good to be home."

"I will get your bags for you and take them to your room."

"Thank you and there are several more bags than we took."

"Honey I will go check on my e-mail. Meet you in the living room."

"My Mrs. Hunt, you look so happy and rested."

"Very happy but not so rested if you know what I mean."

They laughed and went into the house.

What you have plans for you to do today?"

David came out of the bathroom wiping water from his face. "I have to go to the office for a while, but I will be back later then we can go to dinner somewhere tonight. What are you going to do today?"

"Call Charlotte first, she wanted me to call when we got back home."

David put his pants and shirt on. "Sounds like a good day ahead for you." He picked up his brief case and headed for the door.

"What no kiss for me."

"Always a kiss for you. Oh, got to pick Loaner up too." The kiss was just a peck. "Is that the best you can do?" David smiled and kissed her again.

"See you later lover." Denise giggled as she always did.

"Bye lover."

It was around noon when the doorbell rang. Denise brushed her hair back and went to the door. "Hi Charlotte please come." Charlotte as usual well dressed with brief case and note pad came in.

"Denise you look different today."

She bowed her head and smiled. "It was the trip."

"Well let us sit down and tell me all about it."

"The time went by very fast. The hotel was amazing and service great. We ate every day too. The room had a spa in it and room service too, and I have wonderful news but will tell you later."

"A spa in the room, wish I had been there. That is my favorite thing to do." They sat and talked about this and that. Denise looked at Charlotte's scarf. "You have a beautiful scarf."

"Oh this old thing, I have lots of them."

"Me to, I have all colors and flower prints and a clown on one of them."

Charlotte laughed. "Do you mind if I ask you something personal?"

"Sure, what you like to ask?"

"It is about your scar on your neck. Would you show it to me?"

Her hand instantly went to her neck. "My scar on my neck, Why?"

"Well I was thinking that I might be of help. I know a lot about makeup and I want to try something."

Denise slowly removed her scarf from her neck.

Charlotte moved closer to see the scar. "Okay, wait a minute." She opened her purse and took out a bottle of makeup. "Let's try something." She put some on her hand and on the scar and rubbed it in. She sat back and looked. Again she applied more. "Wow, look at it now." Charlotte handed her a mirror.

Denise looked at her and held the mirror up to see. A strange look came to her. "It is almost gone." She kept looking. "It is not the right color for you but we can go shopping for the right color." Denise kept looking.

"When we go, now?"

Charlotte smiled. "Anytime you want."

Suddenly there was a strange noise up stairs. Charlotte heard it and looked at Denise. "Did you hear that? Sound like a glass broke. Is David home?"

"No we are alone. Mildred is off today but I will go see."

"I'll go with you."

"No, I will be right back." Denise headed up the stairs. She looked in the guest bedroom and started to go to her bedroom. As she entered a man dressed in black spun around with a gun holding her diamond bracelet.

He pointed the gun at her. "Well, you must be Mrs. Hunt. You have good taste in your diamonds."

"What are you doing here? That is mine. Give it to me."

"Oh no lady, in fact we are going down stairs and get more things. Turn around and go." He grabbed her arm and they started down the stairs. As they got to the bottom Charlotte turned to see the man and gun.

"What is going on?"

The man shoved Denise into the living room waving his gun. "Shut up lady."

"Denise, are you alright?"

Denise was crying. "He has my diamond bracelet." He waved the gun again.

"And that is not all I'm going to get. Okay pretty lady open the wall safe."

"Don't do it Denise."

He went to Charlotte and put the gun to her head. "You want to die? I told you to shut up. Now open it."

"I cannot, only my husband can do it."

"I have heard that before. Now you have ten seconds to open it or you both die, understand?"

David's car stopped in front of the house. "Okay Loaner, you go do your thing." He got his brief case and cane and started into the house. The door was opened a bit. "That's strange." He went in shouting.

"Honey, I'm home where are you?" As he entered the living room he saw the man with the gun and Denise crying and Charlotte with her hands up.

"What the hell."

The man pointed the gun at him. "Welcome home honey." He laughed as he cocked the hammer back on the gun. "Mr. Hunt, all American millionaire, good to see you again. Now would you be so kind as to open that safe of yours or I may have to shoot all of you. Do it now!"

David shook his cane at the man. "I know you, you did some work on the house six months ago."

"That's right Hunt. Now do as I ask or your wife goes first." He pointed the gun at her.

"Okay, okay, wait a minute." Again he shook the cane at the man. "Only one thing I want to say."

"Oh yeah what is that"

"You're a dead man." David pulled the trigger on the cane hitting the man in the heart. He fell back hard and blood was left on the wall.

David went to Denise. "It is over honey. He can't hurt anyone now."

Charlotte came and hugged them. "Thank you David."

David got his cell phone and dialed 911.

"911 can I help you?"

"Yes, my name is David Hunt and I have just killed a man. Would you have the police come here and an ambulance?"

"Is he dead?"

"Very much so."

It only took minutes till the police cars drove up to the house. Four officers ran in. One searched the house. One went to the man lying on the floor. The detective went to David. "What happen here?"

"He tried to rob us at gun point."

"Where is your gun?"

David handed him the cane.

"What's this?"

"My gun, I had it specially made for me."

"I have never seen this before."

Denise spoke up. "He has my diamond bracelet in his pocket. Can I have it back please?"

"Don't worry mam you will get it back and your cane too sir."

The three of them watched as the ambulance drivers took the man out on a stretcher. The detective watched. "Did you know this man?"

"Know him? No but he did some work here at the house."

"Okay, that will wrap it up here. We will be in touch with some paper work."

"Thank you detective. Have a safe day."

Charlotte gave a sigh of relief. "This is going to make quite a story."

"No story Charlotte, let's keep this to our self." Denise hugged David.

"You just keep on protecting me don't you?"

David hugged her very tight. "I always will sweetheart."

Denise kept thinking about the man with the gun.

"David, do you think he would have shot me and Charlotte?"

"Well sweetheart I could not take that chance." He thought about others that he had killed in the war. It seemed so long ago but he could hear in the back of his mind the Captain saying, "Kill him before he kills you."

"No sweetheart, I could not take that chance when someone might hurt you. You mean too much to me to take that chance." Charlotte came to them. "This is too much excitement for one day, call you later Denise."

"David, I have never been so frightened in my life."

"Well to tell you the truth, it did me to but it is over now."

Now let's make you up...

It was a bright sunny day as the phone rang. Denise went to answer it.

"Chow, I mean hello."

Charlotte laughed over the phone. "Chow to you Denise. Charlotte here, I was wondering if you were free today. Are you? I have some more notes to go over with you and if you want, we could go shopping."

"Wonderful. Yes I am free today. David is out most of today and shopping is always a good thing."

"Okay Hun I will see you soon. Bye or chow." She laughed and hung up.

Denise was excited as she got into the shower. Shopping was her thing and with a friend made the day perfect.

David sat across from the doctor.

"How did it go telling her the news?"

"It wasn't easy. I was so afraid she would take it the wrong way but I got a wonderful, understanding wife."

"Glad to hear that. So, then does she want to start? We can make an appointment for her to come in and I will answer all her questions."

"It should be soon. Just want to prepare her for it. Is next week good for you? That should give me time to talk to her more about it."

"That is a good idea. Don't want to frighten her with details. You know Mr. Hunt this will be a big change for you to. Seeing her with two pretty blue eyes looking back at you, are you ready for this?"

"Glad you brought this up. It will take an adjustment I suppose. I really haven't thought about it too much but just to see her smiling face with two eyes will be worth it."

"David, what about you? I mean you could get another arm if you wanted, maybe even another foot."

"Thought about that too, an arm might be nice but a foot, no I am very comfortable with my cane. I'll think about an arm."

"Anytime you want. I know great people that can help you with that."

"Thanks doc. I'll be in touch about Denise."

It was the drive home that David had trouble with a turn of the car. He pulled over and stopped looking at the steering wheel.

He in passing had thought about another arm. He touched his shoulder and thought of the gunfire that had taken it away from him. It would be nice to hold Denise with two arms again.

Can't see a thing...

It was ten o' clock as Charlotte and Denise pulled into the mall's parking lot. "Great, it's not crowed."

As they went in the air condition building Denise grabbed Charlotte's arm. "Look, scarfs."

"We will get back to that. First let's hit the cosmetic counter."

They sat on stools as a lady came to them.

"Good morning, may I help you?" Charlotte looked at Denise.

"Are you ready for this?" Denise shook her head.

"I think I am frightened." Charlotte took her hand.

"Don't be, just leave things to me. Ah yes, looking for a good makeup to match this ladies skin tone. Show us what you got." Denise smiled at her.

"Okay Hun, hold out your arm and we will match your color." The lady got several shades and put them on the counter. She put a shade on Denise's arm and rubbed it in. Charlotte shook her head.

"Nope, try another shade please." Again the woman applied another shade.

Charlotte again shook her head. "Try this one." She handed it to the sales lady. Denise kept looking at all the shades on her arm. She looked at the lady and at Charlotte. "Can I speak to you over there?" They took a few steps away from the counter. "I am confused Charlotte. It is my neck I want to cover not my arm."

"We want a good shade. I know what I'm doing, just leave it to me."

They went back and sat down. The sales lady looked at them.

"This is not where you want to cover is it?"

"No it is not thank you. It is her neck. She has a scar that needs to be covered."

"In that case let me see the scar. The neck has a different shade to cover."

Denise slowly removed the scarf. Charlotte held her hand.

"Oh I see. It is a little red so it may take two different shades to hide it."

"Two?"

"Yes, one for the skin tone, and one for the scar. That should not be a problem. We will put this one on first then this one."

As she applied the makeup on the scar it started to disappear. Denise watched as the lady put the makeup on. She quickly looked in the mirror.

"It is gone Charlotte, it is gone."

Charlotte laughed and smiled. "Told you I knew what I was doing. We'll take four bottles of both."

At the house Denise kept looking in her mirror. She held it close then far away. She kept smiling as she had not done in quite a while.

"You are a truly great friend. What do you think of my new neck?"

"Well it looks great but you will have to learn how to put it on. Makeup is an art, just look at mine. See how smooth it is. No really honey you look great."

"I cannot wait to show David. He has seen me in so many scarfs. Now I do not have to buy them anymore. This is wonderful. I am so happy."

"You deserve to be happy. You have a great house, clothes, and David."

"You love him to?"

"After what he did a few days ago, yes I do." They lifted their glasses in a toast. "May your days always be happy ones and plenty of makeup."

The laughed and hugged.

Denise sat in front of her dresser looking into the large mirror. She could not believe that the makeup had covered the scar that well. She brushed her long hair back and leaned in for a closer look. Turning her head from side to side her smile was that of a small girl at Christmas time. As she kept looking, the doorbell rang. Happy with herself she opened the door. David stood there with a smile. "Something for Mrs. Denise Hunt." He held up his cane with her diamond bracelet on the end of it.

Her eye widened as she saw the bracelet. "Oh David, you got it back." She took it off the cane and put it on her arm.

They sat in his office. He kept looking at her as she held up her arm admiring the bracelet. "I see you have your cane back too."

He looked at her. There was something different about her but didn't know what it was. All of a sudden she said, "Turn around and close your eyes."

He swiveled around in the chair not knowing what to expect from her. She reached for a rubber band on the desk and put her hair back in a ponytail. She walked around the desk and sat on the corner of it. "Okay David, look at me." He turned to see what she wanted him to see. His mouth opened and his eyes widened.

"You have your hair back in a ponytail. I haven't seen that in a long time."

"And that is not all. See my scar, no more there anymore." Her face was all a glow as he stood looking for the scar.

"Amazing, what did you do?"

"It was my friend Charlotte. She took me to the mall and we got makeup. The lady showed me how to put it on so no more scar can be seen."

"You look like I remember you years ago. Just beautiful and I love your hair pulled back again. This calls for a celebration." She smiled and laughed.

"I have been celebration all day."

Let's do it...

Steak and lobster and a bottle of the best wine sit in front of them. David poured the wine and raised his glass.

"To the most beautiful wife ever."

She raised her glass and touched his glass.

"To the most handsome man ever, my husband."

As the evening went on David leaned over to her. "I saw the doctor."

"What you talk about?"

"You, when would you like to see him and talk to him about your eye?"

"He will tell me everything?"

"Yes and the operation can be done very soon. Just think, you will see again in a matter of months. Maybe in less time."

"This is so sudden you tell me. What must I do?"

"Just have faith in me and the doctor's care."

"I have always trusted in you David. You will be with me all the way?"

"All the way sweet. You think about it and let me know and we will go see him."

She sat staring at the glass of wine. The war had taken away her beautiful and now the thought of undoing that time was about to happen.

"David I think I am ready. I do want to see with both eyes you again."

"That's my girl. I'll make all the arrangements. I love you."

That night she sat again in front of the large mirror looking at her eye. Slowly she took the patch off. She did not remember the building falling on her. She did not remember the glass cutting her neck. She did not remember losing her eye.

She only remembered the pain when she woke up in the hospital and that doctor told her she had lost her eye. Now she was about to get a new start on life with two eyes, something she thought would never happen.

David sat up in the bed. "Honey, are you coming to bed?"

She turned looking at him. He was making all this possible for her. She ran to him. "Oh David, I love you so much. Thank you for all you are doing for me."

"Hey, it is for me too. I want to see the girl I knew long ago and the woman that is here with me now."

The passion of their love was stronger than ever.

"David, make love to me forever as we did long ago."

Long ago was again and better than ever.

It only takes a little while...

A nurse came in and gave the doctor the chart on Denise. He sat looking it over. "Age, birth, color of eyes, husband's name." He looked at them. "Looks like everything is in order. Talk to me Denise. Tell me your thoughts. How you feel about this, what do you expect, all your questions."

She reached for David's hand. "David has made me feel very comfortable about the new eye. It has been so long that I have not seen things that are important for me to see with two eyes again. The sunset, the moon, children playing, and for me this is a blessing from God and my husband."

"Well, let me tell you a few things. First, the operation will be in a clean hospital. I have a staff of doctors that will assist me. The operation will take a few hours and you will not feel any pain whatsoever. After that, you will stay in the hospital for a few days and we will watch for any infections. You have nothing to worry about we have done many of these before. All have been successful. You will then go home and get your rest till I come to your house for your exam. I have talked to David, and there will be a nurse stay with you at all times and dress your eye and give you any pain medicine you may need if any at all. Your rest period will be about a month during this time you will stay out of the sun and wear sunglasses for a while. After that, during my follow-ups, you can go outside and enjoy the sunlight. I will tell you that you will see a milky shade of color and that will go away. You will start to see colors. You will see again, as you always did before."

He looked at her chart.

"Now I have you set for next week. I will be in touch with David where and when. You are a beautiful lady and you will see again."

They sat in the car looking straight ahead. David took her hand and kissed it. "I am very proud of you. You are very strong. That war has made you strong. Never again will I ever let anything hurt you, again."

"I know that and I will always be there for you. You have saved my life and there is no way of repaying you for that."

"Do you feel good about what the doctor said?"

"Yes I do. I feel very good. There is only one thing."

"What's that?"

"Can I eat anything I want?" They started to laugh as they drove off.

"Anything you want sweetheart, anything you want."

A new way of seeing things...

"Denise, Mrs. Hunt, how do you feel?" The doctor leaned over her looking at the bandage.

"Am I alive?"

He smiled and wrote on the chart to give her pain medicine every four hours. "Very much so, everything went very well. Squeeze my hand please. Good."

"My head hurts, and I am thirsty."

"That is normal and now you must rest." He turned to the nurse standing by. "Get her some ice."

"Yes sir."

"Denise I will check in on you again soon, so sleep now." He turned to David. "You have a strong willed girl there. She will be just fine." The doctor left the room. David went to her and kissed her and held her hand.

"Honey, I am right here." She was asleep.

It was a long ride home for David. All he could do was done, now it was up to Denise to pull through. He kept thinking about what the doctor had said. "She is a strong willed girl." He knew this from her actions that she had taken about her scar. She had done something about that. It had bothered her for a long time. She did not like to wear all the scarfs all the time everywhere she went and he knew this. He also knew that the patches she wore were a great bother to her. He also knew that the new eye would make her a new person. This made him very happy that he had helped her get it.

As he pulled into the driveway, Loaner came barking and jumping around the car. "Hi boy, looking for Denise? Well she will be home soon."

Mildred met him at the door. "How is she Mr. Hunt?"

With cane in hand he went inside. "She is doing fine but in a little pain."

"Can I do anything for her? Can I go see her sir?"

"She would like that but give her a few more days."

She dusted some more. "Sure do miss her, not much to do around here without her here. She helps me make the bed and waters the flowers and even cooks me lunch."

"Yeah me too, but she will be coming home soon then you will have to be there for her. That will give you lots to do then." He went in his office as he heard her say. "Sure do miss her." As he sat looking out the bay windows, he could see her playing with Loaner throwing a ball. She loved to do that.

He closed his eyes and started to pray. "God, you have given her again to me, now stand by her side and help her with the new life that is ahead of her. Ease her pain and give her the strength she needs now. I pray to you because I know you know I love her with all my heart and need her, amen."

It was her second day in the hospital as the doctor took the bandage off of her. Two other doctors were standing by the bed watching as he put drops on the eye lid. She blinked and squeezed the nurse's hand.

"Did that hunt Denise?"

"Not really, it feels cool."

"Well it looks normal to me." He turned to the other doctors. "The redness will take a few more days to start going down and so will the swelling but as you can see everything else is normal." He turned to the nurse. "How did she sleep last night?"

"She had some pain, but slept well. Only once did she wake up. At that time she called for water and as you had said, I gave her some ice."

Denise moved her legs and turned her head.

"Doctor Bain, when I can go home?"

"If you feel better and no pain, soon. I do like what I see and the drops will help your eyelid to stay soft and help the eye to become stable. As I see it now, I should be able to test the eye in a matter of time."

"What is test the eye you say?"

"That is when you open the eye so I can see more. See if you can see any light that I will shine in your eye. You should be able to see light." He again turned to the other doctors. "Any questions gentlemen." There were none.

The nurse stayed. "Mrs. Hunt, I will be here if you need anything."

As the doctors were leaving Charlotte was standing there and came into the room. "Hey girl, how do you feel today?"

Denise saw her and tried to smile. "Today I have small pain."

Charlotte went to her and smiled. She held up a bag and waved it in the air. "I got you something."

Denise raised her hand wanting to hold Charlotte's hand. Charlotte grabbed her hand and Denise held her hand tight.

"You are so good to me my friend."

"Well that is what friends do for each other. Buy things." She laughed.

"Look what I brought you." She reached in the bag and brought out a hand full of hair brushes. "What color do you like? Got you one for each day, and some ties so you can wear your hair back anyway you like. Plus."

She reached into the bag and came out with several bottles of makeup.

"These bottles of makeup, oh yes." Again she reached into the bag.

"Some perfume to make you smell good. I like this one." She took the bottle and dabbed some behind Denise's ear and touched her nose. "Like it?" Denise wiggled her nose and took the bottle of perfume looking at it.

"Very much. I have never smell so good." They both laughed.

"I thank you for all this presents and for coming to see me my friend."

David knocked on the door and came in with two dozen roses behind him back. He went to Denise with a big kiss. He stood looking at her.

"How do you feel today sweetheart?"

"Much better than yesterday. I miss you last night."

"I missed you to. I brought you these to cheer you up." He brought the roses from behind him.

"Oh they are beautiful."

Charlotte leaned over to smell. "Oh yeah, these are true love flowers. Wish someone would give me some."

"I'm sorry, hi Charlotte, good to see you again. Thanks for being here."

"No problem David, she is my friend."

"David, look at the things she brought for me. Did you smell me to?"

"Sure did. You smell like fresh cut grass, like mountain air, like.."

"We get the picture David." Charlotte smiled.

"Okay Denise, David, got to run, things to do, so I'll see you later Denise."

"Thank you again Charlotte for everything. I love the perfume."

"Glad you do honey. See ya'll. Bye."

David waved as she left the room. "So, I saw the doctor in the hall and he seemed very happy with you."

"He is so nice to me. I am happy with him to."

David laughed. "You should be. He cost enough but he is the best too."

"You have to pay him a lot?"

"Not enough for what he is doing for you. Besides, we have plenty of money enough to take you to dinner when you get out of here and take another trip somewhere. Think about where you want to go. I hear that California is great this time of the year. See movie stars, see the ocean."

"Where is California? I have heard of that place."

"About four thousand miles from here on the other coast, west coast."

"You have been there? That is long drive."

"No drive. We will fly in big airplane."

"You fly us there?"

David laughed. "Nope, we will sit in first class seats drinking champagne all the way."

"I love champagne. Been a long time since I drank champagne."

"Nothing but the best for my girl. I love you. Do you love me?"

"Silly man, you know I do, very much. I love you. I love you."

He leaned and kissed her. He brushed her hair back and stood looking at her.

"It won't be long now till I can hold you in my arm with a kiss."

"Soon maybe, the doctor say he like what he see in my eye."

"I love what I see in your eye. The woman I have dreamed of."

"You say the right thing I need to hear David. Thank you for the roses. They mean so much to me, and when you not here, I will see your face."

The time went by slow some days and fast others. A week had passed for Denise as the nurse stood by her bed. "Good morning Mrs. Hunt." She refilled the water pitcher. "Comment sont vous?"

Denise looked at her. "I didn't know you speak French, merci, very well thank you."

"I checked in on you last night and you sleep all night. That's good."

"Yes, the pain is very small. In fact I feel much better but one thing."

"Yes, what is that?"

"I am very hungry."

The nurse laughed. "That is a very good sign. I'll get your breakfast now."

Denise sat up in bed eating her breakfast when the doctor came in.

"Morning. That looks good. Eggs over easy, toast, coffee, makes me hungry. How do you feel today?" He looked at her chart.

"I see here on your chart that you slept well and did not ask for any pain medicine. Good sign. Eat your breakfast and I'll be back to check on you. Glad to see you up. Good sign." He left the room.

She drank her coffee and lay down thinking what he had said. She rolled over looking at the roses. "It won't be long now David, not too long."

The nurse came in and got the tray. "You ate everything good for you. I will be leaving for today but another nurse will be here soon. You need anything before I leave?"

"No, I am fine."

"Okay, au revoir pour maintenant and ayez une bonne journe'e."

"You to and merci."

France and the French people she missed very much.

It made her feel good to say French words to the nurse and to hear them said back to her. At home David would once in a while speak French to her but his French was not that good. She would laugh at him then kiss him and say, "It is okay, I understand you."

An hour had passed when the doctor came back into the room with the other doctors. "Well let's see." He took the chart and showed the other doctors what had happen the night before. The other nurse came in and stood by the doctor. "Can I be of help doctor?" He handed her the chart and turned to Denise. "Yes you can. Get clean bandages ready and stand by." He looked at Denise. "You look great today, ready for the test? It won't take long."

She turned on her back and lay there waiting. The other doctors gathered around the bed. The nurse came in with bandages and the eye drops. The doctor bent over Denise and started to remove the bandage from her face.

"This may hurt a little bit so try not to open your eyes okay." The doctors were taking notes as he started to remove the bandages slowly.

Slowly he peeled the bandage off. Denise did not move. The nurse was holding her hand. "Now did that hurt you?" Denise shook her head.

"Hand me the drops please." He dropped several drops on your eye and dabbed her face. He looked at the other doctors. "Now doctors take note of all this as I start the test." He got the small flashlight out of his bag.

"Now Denise, with your eyes closed, I will shine the light in your eye and tell me if you see anything." He shined the light in her eye moving it from side to side. "See anything?" She blinked her eyes a few times slowly.

"Would you do it again for me please?" Again he did the same thing.

"Anything?"

"I think there was light moving across."

"That's good. Now I want you to try to open your new eye but keep the other closed okay. Now the pain you will feel will be your eyelid not your eye. The eyelid has some redness in it that has not healed as yet. Now when I tell you, very slowly try to open the eye." He looked at the doctors writing.

"Okay Denise, slowly open the eye the best you can." Bombs bursting in the air all around her went thought her mind. She relaxed and thought of David. Slowly she tried to open the eye. There was pain but she kept trying. The eye slowly opened. The doctor quickly looked at the eye and again turned the flashlight on. He waved it across her face. "I see a light but not clearly."

"Close your eye slowly now, that's it very slow. Good." He put more drops on the eye and covered it with the bandage. "Wonderful Denise, just wonderful."

He stood up looking at the doctors. "We have done a great job doctors."

He leaned down and kissed Denise. "You have done a great job to." She had a tear run down her face. He wiped it away. "Not to cry, it is all right."

She reached for his hand. "Will I see again? Will you say yes or no to me?"

"I will tell you one thing for sure. You can go home very soon and I will test the eye again but I can tell you now, yes, you will see again."

She squeezed his hand tight. He squeezed her hand and kissed her again.

"Would you like anything before I go?"

"No sir, can I call David and tell him?"

"You don't have to call he is in the hall waiting to come to see you. Gentlemen shall we move on? Splendid, excellent work here." The doctors left the room. David stopped Doctor Bain in the hall as he was leaving.

"Tell me doctor, is she, will she, I mean please tell me the truth."

"She is a wonderful woman. You will have a great life together. Yes David she will see again with both eyes I am sure, but it will take time."

"How long will it take?"

"Maybe three months, maybe less. You will have to take care of her then we will see. I will be seeing you both soon. Have a good day."

My prayer was answered...

David watched him walk down the hall and turn the corner. It was then it hit him what he had said. "She will see again, with both eyes."

He burst in the room with a big smile. "Did you hear the news?"

She sat up in your bed. "What news David?"

"It is about your eye."

"Well, yes I am here when the doctor tell me." David hit his head.

"Of course, I mean I am so excited about you and what he told me."

The head nurse came in. "Hi Hun. How are you feeling?" She looked at the chart. "I see the doctor has you scheduled for you x-ray in one hour. First let's put the drops in your eye."

"Tell me, what do the drops do for my eye?"

"They lubricate the eye and the eyelid so you can blink. It also takes the redness out of your eye. You know, like you been in the sun too long your eyes dry out and burn or you drink too much gin and you get blood shot eyes. Well this is lubrication it takes the redness out of the eyes." She turned to David. "You drink sir? Your eyes are a little red."

"Ah, not today, just tired, not enough sleep lately."

"Maybe she put drops in your eyes David."

"No that's alright."

The nurse took the bandage off and put the drops in Denise's eye. Again she looked at the chart. "Oh, it says here, no more bandages just use patch. I'll go get you a few. Tan be alright? I'll be back in a minute honey."

David watches her leave. "Are my eyes red?" He bent over to Denise and kissed her. "More flowers for my lady."

"Oh they are so pretty. That is good news no? No more bandage."

"That is the best news ever. No more bandages."

The nurse came back. "Here you go honey, I'll be back in a half hour to get you, okay? Then we'll put the patch on you before the x-ray is taken. Excuse me sir."

"You will stay with me David?"

"Every step of the way sweetheart, every step of the way." She sat back in the bed. David adjusted the pillow for her.

"Would you hand me that notebook over there?" He gave it to her.

"I write poem for you." She turned the page and started reading. "David loves me this I know, for my bible tells me so. His arm is strong, I know he cares, he protects me always, and his love he shares."

David did not know what to say to her. With tears in his eyes he finally said the words she wanted and needed to hear. "I love you so very, very much."

"Okay honey, come to mama." The nurse rolled the wheelchair around the bed.

David walked to the bed. "Here honey, let me help you."

"Hey mister let me do my job."

David sat down. "Ah, yes mam, sorry." The nurse rolled Denise out of the room.

The x-ray room was very cold. "Need a blanket honey?"

"I will be okay thank you." The tech came out from the glass wall.

"Mrs. Hunt?"

"Yes."

"Let me see your armband. Yep that's you. Let's get started. Tell you what we are going to do. I will take pictures of your eye from different angles."

She rolled the chair over to the x-ray machine. Just stay seated okay. She adjusted the machine in front of Denise's eye. "Now I will tell you when I'm going to take the picture so hold your breath and don't move at all." Denise watched her go behind the glass wall. "Okay, hold your breath and don't move. It will only take a second. Ready?" Denise heard the machine click. The lady came and adjusted the machine again. "Okay, the same thing again." She disappeared around the wall again. "Ready? Hold your breath and don't move." The machine clicked again. "Just sit tight, want to check the photos."

Denise looked around the cold room. "Don't you get cool in here?" The girl laughed. "I have been here so long it doesn't bother me anymore." She came out from the wall. "Okay sweet, you are finished. You can go now." The nurse was called and came to wheel her back to her room.

"Did it hurt?"

"What hurt?"

"The machine, I have had patients pass out in there. Just kidding with you honey."

"You are mean lady. Bad jokes are not fun. I tell doctor your bad joke."

"Well, I am sorry Mrs. Hunt but around sick people a joke does good."

"Well just drive nurse and do not break speed limit."

"Ah, yes mam. Sorry about that." Denise laughed at what she had said.

"Just kidding as you like to say, just kidding."

David stood as they came into the room. He watched the nurse put her back in bed. "Sir, I'm sorry about jumping on you while ago."

"That okay, I know you have a tough time around here."

Denise spoke up. "She is bad nurse. She say people die in here."

"Did you say that to my wife?" Denise giggled and laughed.

"Just kidding with her, just kidding her David." David threw a book at her. "Silly girl, you learn too much to fast here."

Charlotte popped her head in. "Anyone home?" Denise and David were laughing at what Denise had said.

"Yep we are here."

Charlotte came in and hugged Denise. "Look what I brought you, ice cream, butter pecan."

"Oh that is my favorite cream, Thank you. You are so kind. Merci."

"So, what's the news around here?"

"The doctor check me and see, no bandage. He say I look good. I had x-ray of my eye today and I am doing good."

"Wonderful. How about you David? How are you holding up?"

"Well first, you didn't bring me anything, but I'll get by thank you."

"Oh you poor thing." She reached in the bag and handed him a pint of his favorite strawberry ice cream. A big smile came to him.

"You remembered. I love this kind of ice cream."

"And a spoon to." She turned to Denise.

"Any news when you can get out of here?"

"Maybe he say a few days, I cannot wait. I miss my home."

"I bet you do. This place is depressing after a while."

David stood up. "Got to go sweetheart but will be back later."

Charlotte went to Denise with a hairbrush. "You need a hair brushing."

"Okay girls, you play makeup and look pretty for me when I get back."

"Hey lover boy, I'm always pretty." Denise laughed.

"She is right. She always pretty." David left the room.

"Okay, sit up straight." She started to brush Denise's hair back.

"I wish I had long hair. Use to but it was so hot I had to cut it all off."

"Maybe I should cut my hair off like you did."

"You do and David would kick your butt. Besides, you can wear it all ways."

"Tell me something. Why you no have a husband? You are beautiful."

"Long story sweet. Did at one time but he left me for another woman."

"Are you hurt over that?" She smiled.

"Not anymore. Now I just play the field and all the bars. Sit still."

"Field? I do not understand. What is field?"

"Don't worry kid, you want have to play the field or bars." She handed Denise a mirror. She turned her head from side to side looking.

"Do you think I will be pretty with two eyes?"

Charlotte laughed loudly. "Tell you what, I'll take a before and after picture of you and you tell me."

"Before what?"

Charlotte hit her on her head with the brush. "I see why David calls you silly. You are silly girlfriend." She smiled. "Okay honey I have to go and run, got to see a publisher friend of mine."

"Will you see me again later?"

"Count on it." She got her thing and headed for the door and turned.

"Chow."

Denise lay back in bed looking at herself in the mirror. "Chow."

A new day breaks...

It was raining in New York and the clouds were thick. The small radio was on and the weatherman was saying, "Yep, all day and tomorrow too." She looked out the window and remembered the rain in France. It seemed different here in this crowed city. People were running to get out of it. In France they would just sit at a café and enjoy the rain. She wondered where

David was. Was he running in the rain? Did he have an umbrella?

David came into the room fast. He went straight to her.

"Are you alright? The doctor called my cell and said to come to the hospital this morning that he needed to talk to me."

"I am fine, see my hair pulled back, you like?"

"Yes I like. You sure you are alright?"

Doctor Bain came in. "Sorry I'm late, it's a mess out there."

"I got your call, you said for me to get here fast. I was worried about her."

The doctor sat on the bed. "How are you today?" David pulled up a chair.

He opened the chart and ran his finger down the page.

"The reason I wanted you here was to talk to you both. Now for the good news. The x-rays show me that the eye has adjusted to the body and the body has accepted the new eye. The swelling has gone down and that is good news for me, you never know about these things. So, the better news is, you can go home later today. That is if you want to." David jumped in the air. Denise lay back on the bed with a big smile and laughed. "Now David the nurse will stay with both of you till I say she can go. She will help in giving the drops to your eye and in any way you need her. The other part of this, and listen to me Denise, is you must stay out of bright sun light and you must wear the patches given to you till I say you don't have to, understand?" He put the chart back on the end of the bed. "Any questions before I go?" They looked at each other. "Okay, I will set a time to come to your house and see you."

"Thank you doctor for everything."

"Don't thank me, thank God for looking over my shoulder." He laughed and left the room. David went to Denise and hugged her tight. She whispered in his ear. "Thank God and you."

"I'll call Mildred and let her know the news."

"Can you also call Charlotte and tell her for me. She will be happy for me."

"Not as happy as I am. Yes sweetheart, I'll call her too."

"When you call Mildred, ask if she make me food. I am very hungry."

"Sure will, and tonight we will go out and have a good steak and wine."

It may not have been the most loveable night but they didn't care.

"Tomorrow is a new day for the rest of our lives baby." He didn't know what to do first he was so excited. He stood in the hall thinking. It came to him. He took out his cell phone and started making calls.

"Mildred, she is coming home later today."

"That is wonderful. When and what time?"

"I will check her out about five thirty this evening. Now this is what I want you to do. Get a big cake. Five layers. Order wine and champagne, three of each and have them delivered by four thirty. Call your friends, tell them to come. Decorate the house with ribbons and big bows. And big sign that says, "Welcome Home" you know what to do. See you later bye."

"Hello Charlotte, call me when you get this message. She's coming home."

He stood thinking. Flowers, I can do that. His cell rang and sang the song. "Hello, hi glad you got my message. She is coming home today at six. Want you to be at the house about five, can you do that?"

"Great, bring all your friends, it will be a coming home party for her. Say what? Yeah do that. Okay Charlotte see you then." He looked at the phone. "Damn, I wish I had more friends."

The rain had stopped with only a few dark clouds floating by as he sat in his car. He wanted this to be a special night for her coming home. He looked at his watch. It was three. Only two more hours until they would be checking out of the hospital. He walked quickly back into the hospital. A nurse was standing at the counter on the floor where Denise was. "Hi."

"Hi Mr. Hunt has the rain stopped?"

"Ah yes. Say, you know my wife right?"

"Sure we all love her. I heard she will be leaving."

"That's what I want to talk to you about. You think you could get all the nurses to come to a party for her tonight about five. She would really love to have all you guys there. Yeah, a coming home party."

"I will see what I can do. I will for sure. Let me see."

She looked at the chart. "Yep your address is right here. I'll tell everyone."

"Great, see you later." He thought about Denise. A dress and shoes. Quickly he went to his car and drove home. He was going through her clothes looking for a dress and shoes for her. "Ah, I like this." He hurried down the stairs to the car again. Everything had to be just right. He sat thinking about what to do next. The flowers he thought.

As he went into the flower shop, a lady came to him. "Can I help you?"

"Yes please. I would like two dozen red roses and some of those."

He looked around the shop. "And a bunch of those to." She started to gather the flowers. "Anything else sir?" He handed her a hundred dollar bill.

"No thanks, keep the change." He turned and went to the door. On the way to the car he saw a man sitting on the front of his car. As he got closer he saw that the man was dressed in a black leather jacket and a motorcycle stood beside the car. "Can I help you?" The man turned looking at him.

"Oh pretty flowers, they for your pretty wife? Your name is Hunt right?"

"That's right. How do you know my wife?" The man laughed.

"I don't know her yet but I will soon."

"What does that mean? What do you want?" The man got off the car and got on his motorcycle and started it up. "You'll see Hunt. See you later." With that he rode off into the darkness. David stood wondering what that was about. How did he know Denise? He put his cane and flowers in the car.

It was four thirty as David carried the dress and shoes into the lobby of the hospital. A nurse waved. "See you later." He went to Denise's room.

"Hi honey, look what I got for you to wear home."

"Oh, I like." A nurse came in the room. "Mr. Hunt, I am Sandy Burns. I am the nurse that will be taking care of Denise for a while at your home."

"Glad to meet you Sandy. Can you help her with these clothes?"

"Sure thing Mr. Hunt." She laid them on the bed as Denise took off her robe.

"Oh David I am so glad to be going home. I miss everything there."

"Well it won't be long now sweetheart and we have missed you too."

"Isn't Sandy sweet? and she very pretty to. You think so?"

"Sure do. I'm going to check you out of here. Be back in a minute."

"We will be ready when you get back Mr. Hunt."

"Thanks Sandy, be right back." David stood in the hall thinking about what the biker had said. "I don't know her yet but I will soon." He didn't like what he had heard or the way he had said it.

"Just sign here Mr. Hunt. I'll get a wheelchair for her."

"That has been taken care of, thank you for your help."

"Ok Mr. Hunt, hope to see you later. We love Denise around here."

"Yeah, she is a very special lady." He went back to the room. Denise came to him with a big hug. "How do I look?" He stood back looking at her.

"You are as pretty as hay in a field." She laughed and kissed him.

"Ready?" Sandy rolled the chair to her. "Yes sir, we are ready."

It was getting dark as the three of them got into the warm car. David turned to her. "I love you." He looked at his watch. "Here we go."

Surprise...

As they pulled up to the house Denise looked all around.

"Why is the house so dark? You no pay light bill?"

Sandy laughed. "She is a trip isn't she? I bet you two have lots of fun together."

"That we do."

"Is Loaner here?" That is our dog."

"Yeah, somewhere, let's go in. Want to keep you out of this weather."

"Sandy, I no need chair, I can walk okay."

David opened the door and turned the light on in the hallway. They walked into the living room and he turned the lights there. Everyone jumped out.

"Surprise, welcome home." Denise's mouth opened wide as she saw all the people. Mildred had decorated the room with a big banner and ribbons everywhere. Denise stood with a tear in her eye and waved at all the people.

Charlotte ran to her. "Welcome home." All the nurses gathered around Denise giving her hugs and kisses. She did not know what to say to them.

"I am very happy to come home to all my friends here to see me."

Mildred turned the music on and the party started. Denise kissed David.

"You make all this for me"

"Kind of, with the help of all your friends." Charlotte came with her friend.

"Denise, David, I would like you to meet Kevin Helms. He publishes books and wanted to meet you." David extended his hand. "Nice to meet you." Denise leaned and kissed his cheek. "Me too Mr. Kevin, welcome." He kissed her cheek. "I have heard much about you Denise."

"I hope it was good things."

"Very good things and maybe we can get together and talk about your book. Charlotte has shown me a few notes that were very interesting."

"Charlotte is very interesting herself."

David spoke up. "The bar is open. Let's have a drink shall we."

Everyone was having a good time as the night was coming to an end. Some of the nurses came to Denise saying they had to go and that they had a great time with her while she was in the hospital. Others to had to leave. Denise, David and Sandy sat in the quite living room as the soft music played. "Such a wonderful evening David. The room is beautiful."

"Sandy, there is a guest room next to Denise's room you can stay in."

He slowly stood with his cane. "And you should get your rest sweet."

"Mrs. Hunt, I will put the drops in your eye before you go to sleep."

"Thank you Sandy. I am tired and sleepy. David you coming?"

"Not just yet. I have some work to do in the office. You go ahead."

"Good night Mr. Hunt."

"Good night Sandy." He watched as they went up the stairs. He went into his office, put his cane on the desk and sat down. The door shut. He looked up and saw the biker standing there.

"Nice little party you had here." The biker stood with a grin.

"All those nurses, pretty nurses. Makes me sick."

"How did you get in here? What do you want?"

"You love her very much don't you? I loved someone very much one time."

"Money? Is that what you want?"

"No but I'll take it. What I want is revenge, and eye for an eye." He laughed.

"Funny ain't it, an eye for an eye. You killed my brother with that cane."

"How did you know that?"

"Oh I have my ways."

"I have a hundred thousand dollars in my safe. Take it and go away."

"Let us go get it Mr. Hunt. Leave that cane here. Let's go."

They went to the living room and David went to the safe. He opened it and started to reach in. "Hold on there. Step back don't want any surprises." He stepped back as the man went to the safe. "Oh cute, a gun." He took it and put it in his leather jacket. He took the metal box out and opened it. He stood looking at the money. "Fifty grand for me and fifty for the man I have to pay off. Thank you Mr. Hunt, you made my day, almost."

"What does that mean you bastard?"

"You love your wife, I loved my brother. Think about it. See you later."

He left the house. David heard the motorcycle drive off. David went to his office and grabbed his cell phone. He dialed a number.

"Captain Miller speaking."

"Miller, this is David Hunt. You said the records were sealed about the shooting and no one could get to them. Well some biker knows everything."

"Hold on Mr. Hunt, what are you talking about?"

"The man I killed. Hi brother was here and knows everything about the shooting, about the cane, where I live and about my wife."

"Those records are sealed. Only myself and my assistant know about it."

"Well you have a leak somewhere. He took a hundred thousand dollars from me and said he had to pay some guy off with fifty thousand of it."

"Let me check this out. I'll get right back with you."

"You better. He wants to kill my wife."

The captain pushed the button on the phone. "Get in here now!"

Two armed guards stood outside the captain's door. Kline walked in.

"What's up chief?" The captain sat at his desk. "You, that's what."

The captain was angry.

"Put your gun and badge on my desk." He did as he was told.

"What's wrong? What is this all about?"

The captain stood and went to him.

"Who was that man in here while ago? that biker?"

"I don't know him."

The captain stood and went to him. He patted Kline's suit pocket. He reached in and pulled out an envelope. "What have we here?"

He opened it and started to count the money. "About fifty thousand dollars." He knocked on the door. The officers came in and stood waiting.

"Cuff him and take him away and book him. I'll do the paperwork later. Get me a squad car and three armed officers." They took him away.

David sat for an hour looking at the open safe. He kept tapping his cane on the floor. All he could hear was, "An eye for an eye."

A window in the kitchen broke. He stood and headed to the sound. The biker opened the door holding a gun. "Back again Mr. Hunt. Sit down." Sandy and Denise heard the window break and started down the stairs. As they got to the bottom Denise called out. "David, are you alright?" They walked into the living room and saw the man with the gun. "Go back." David yelled.

"No, no, no, girls come on in. In fact you are the one I came to see." David reached for his cane. "Not this time mister." Sandy put her arm around Denise. "Hey nurse, you can put your arm around me if you want." He pointed the gun at Denise. "Now Mr. Hunt, you can watch her die the way you killed my brother." He cocked the hammer back.

"Why are you doing this? I gave you all the money I had."

He turned to David. "Revenge for what you did."

The front door burst opened and the captain and the officers with their gun drawn came rushing in. "Drop the gun, now! Now!" The biker turned pointing his gun at them. A blast of gunfire echoed through the house. The man fell over a chair and on to the floor dead. Denise ran to David.

"It is alright now. It is over." The captain turned to the officers. "Call for an ambulance and cover him up. Are you two all right? I came to tell you about the leak in my office. It was Kline, and when I saw the motorcycle in the drive I knew he must be in here. Gad this is over with." David shook his hand. Sandy came to Denise. "Come with me Mrs. Hunt." They walked away holding each other. "Thank you captain, for everything."

"You are very welcome Mr. Hunt. It looks like we took a bad guy off the streets and a bad cop in jail for a very long time. It is a good day."

David sat staring at where the man had died. He smiled as he got up with cane in hand and started slowly up the stairs.

"Denise honey, I'm coming to you."

Sandy sat on the edge of the bed holding Denise's hand as David walked in. Sandy again put a cold cloth on Denise's head.

"Honey, are you alright?"

"My head hurts very badly."

Sandy looked at him. "I have to call the doctor will you stay with her a minute?"

"Sure, of course."

She went out and closed the door and dialed his number. "Doctor Bain, this is Sandy at the Hunt house. I think you should come as quickly as you can, it is Mrs. Hunt."

"What happen? Is she all right?"

"She is having very bad headaches."

"Did she fall?" Sandy explained briefly what had happen that night.

"I'll be right there."

It was a matter of ten minutes as the doctor arrived. Mildred walked upstairs with him. "She is in here sir." Quickly he went to the bed as Sandy was putting another cold cloth on Denise's head.

"Any change? David would you wait outside please."

"Only she is shaking more than before." He opened his black bag and took out his stethoscope and put it to her heart. He opened her good eye.

"Roll her sleeve up." Sandy watched as he injected a needle into her arm.

"She in a state of shock, go get me ice, lots of it."

"Yes sir." He took her wrist and counted her heartbeats. Sandy returned.

"Keep ice on her head and arms." He stood shaking his head.

David stood in the hallway waiting. The doctor came to him.

"How is she doctor?"

The doctor looked at him. "Let's go sit down."

They went down stairs into David's office.

"David, it is not good. She is in a state of shock from what has happen."

"Shock?"

"Yes, the body and the nerve system are a strange combination. Sandy has told me what happened. What Denise saw was a man point a gun at her and was about to kill her. It took a while for that to register in her mind. When it did, the nerve system shut down and fear took over her mind. Now I have given her a shot that will make her sleep. A deep sleep and hopefully relax her mind and her nerves. I hate to tell you this but she may lose her eye."

"Her eye?"

"Yes, it is the nerves in her eye that I am concerned about. They are not that strong yet. It will take a while till I can see if they are strong enough."

"What can I do?"

"Pray for her, just pray. That is what I will be doing."

Sandy had ice on Denise and sat watching her. The doctor came in and sat on the bed. He felt of her face and hands.

"Sandy she must sleep and not be disturbed in any matter. Call me if there are any changes. If she ask for David, just hold her hand and let her know you are there with her."

"And can David see her?"

"Not just yet. He is in a little shock that he is not aware of. I'll give him something to help him before I leave. Just watch her closely."

"Yes sir."

David took two of the pills that the doctor gave him and sat back in the chair behind his desk. He closed his eyes and before long he was asleep.

Charlotte came rushing into the house. "Mildred, where is she?"

Mildred shook her head. "She is not good Ms. Charlotte."

"I want to see her. Where is David?"

"He is sleeping in his office." She went into the office and saw him. She sat down. "Oh David, you have had it bad too. I am here to help you all I can."

Upstairs, Denise moaned in her sleep and called for David. Sandy rubbed her hand and arm. "I am here with you Denise, you are safe."

Several hours had passed as David slowly opened his eyes. The first thing that went through his mind was the sight of the gunman pointing the gun at Denise. "No," he shouted as he sat up in the chair. He thought of the pain she had gone through and her new eye. He got up and went up to see her. He knocked on the door softly. Sandy opened the door.

"Can I see her a minute?"

"I'm sorry Mr. Hunt, she is sleeping and must get her rest."

"Yes her rest. I understand but can I touch her?" Sandy opened the door for him to come in. She watched as he stood looking down at her sleeping. He knelt down by the bed and took her hand. He started to cry and prayed.

"God what have I done to you to have made this happen to her? Why must you keep her in pain? Why God, why? Have we not served you? I ask not for myself but for her, give her the strength to overcome this. She is all I have on this earth. I beg you Lord to hear me. Give her back to me."

Sandy came to him and rested her hand on his shoulder.

"God hears all prayers. I know he has heard your prayer. The bible has said, "Therefore I say unto you, anything you pray for in my name, believe, and you will receive."

He looked up at her with tears flowing down his face and smiled.

"You really think so?" She smiled at him as an angel.

"I know so." He looked at her in a strange way.

It was late evening and again the doctor sat on the bed checking for signs that he hoped for. Sandy stood watching him check her heart. He stood and reached into his black bag and took out a small bottle.

"She should be coming around soon. Give her a pain pill and one of these."

"Yes sir. Can she have some food?"

"Yes tomorrow. Now she needs plenty of rest now. The nerve must relax."

He put everything in his bag and went to the door.

"I'll be back early in the morning. Do you need anything?"

"No sir, I'm fine for now." He went to talk to David in the living room. David stood as he came in.

"How is she?"

"I will know more tomorrow when I see her. David, you said you wanted to help. When you talk to her, you must assure her about the man and the gun. You must tell her that he was not going to shoot her or kill her. She needs to hear that. Also tell her that he was not going to hurt you either. This will make her more relaxed about this whole thing if she hears it from you. She trusts in you very much. David, I know this has been hard on you too. You have been very strong through this and she will see this. Understand?"

"I do doctor, and I will do anything I can to make her happy again."

"Good. Also let her sleep. This will help her a lot right now. I might add that you should get as much sleep as you can. You'll need it in days to come."

"Thanks but I'm fine."

"No you are not. You may feel you are but I know better, I'm a doctor."

He left and went to his car and drove away.

It was the longest night ever for David. Getting the home-coming party together, the gunman, the police, the bullets flying, and Denise. He thought about what she would do, if she lost the eye that she wanted so bad.

It was eleven o'clock when he drifted off to sleep. Sandy came down from Denise's room and saw him lying on the couch asleep. She went to him and put a blanket over him. It was then she saw a long throwing knife strapped to his leg. She knew then that he could and would have killed the man. She said to herself, "You are quite a man Mr. Hunt, a man every woman wants."

The day after...

The rain had stopped and went away. It was the second day he had not seen Denise or talked to her and it was killing him.

Loaner came in and lay at his side. "Hi boy." Loaner wagged his tail. "You hungry?" David sat up on the couch rubbing his head. "Come on boy, I'll feed you." Sandy came into the room as he got up.

"Mr. Hunt are you alright?"

"Yes just a little tired. Too much sleep I think."

"Do you feel like seeing Denise? She has been asking for you and will not take no for an answer. It may do her some good to see you."

"Now, now can I see her?"

"Yes I am sure the doctor would approve."

He got his cane and smiled. "Just what I have been waiting for."

The door opened and he stood looking at her lying there in bed. Slowly and calmly he went to her and sat on the bed. She moved a little.

"Honey, I am here." She opened her eye slowly.

"I knew you would come to me. David," He stopped her from talking.

"Not another word sweetheart, I have something to say." He held her hand.

"The other night was a terrible night for you. I know, it was for me too but I want to tell you that that man did not want to hurt you in any way. He only wanted to scar our love. He wanted revenge on something, anything. He wanted to scare me by pointing that gun at you. He was not going to shoot you. It was me he was after not you. Honey I would give my life for you."

"What would I do without you? You are my life, my breath, my soul."

"You must believe what I have said. It was me, not you, he wanted."

"I do believe you my husband, I do believe." She closed her eye.

"I believe."

Sandy came in. "Maybe she should sleep now. I will stay with her."

"Yes of course. Maybe later can I come back?"

"Maybe later when she wakes up." David left the room.

The doorbell rang and Mildred answered it. "Is Mr. Hunt in?"

"Yes he is, please wait." She went to tell him someone was at the door.

"Captain Miller, please come in."

"I was in the neighborhood and wanted to stop and give you this." He handed David a large package. David opened it.

"My hundred thousand dollars. Thank you very much."

"Thought you may need it." He smiled with a chuckle. "Just need you to sign this paper that you received it."

"Will do."

"Yeah, don't want this much cash to lay around the office."

David laughed. "Why? You have crooks there?" They shook hands.

"Okay my friend, got to catch the bad guys. Good luck sir."

David went to the safe and put it in there. The doorbell rang again.

"I'm sorry but I didn't ask about your wife. How's she doing?"

"We are hoping for the best. She had a nervous breakdown."

"I can understand that. Someone points a gun at me I would too. Sure hope she gets over it. Can I come by some time and check on her?"

"She would like that. Thanks for your concern."

Several hours had passed. Sandy sat reading the newspaper. She looked over and saw Denise trying to set up. She went to her.

"Denise honey, are you alright?"

"I do not know. My mouth is very dry and I am very hungry to."

"Here is some ice water." Denise drank it all.

"More please and food too, please."

"That makes me feel good for you to ask for food."

"Why? You hungry too?"

Sandy laughed at her. "No, but I will have Mildred make you something. Coming right up honey."

"Maybe a bottle of wine, a big bottle."

"No, no wine yet, it would not be good with your medicine." She stood up. "Tell you what, I will brush you hair for you."

"I look bad don't I? I feel much better than I did."

"I'll be right back, you stay in bed okay."

"I must use the bathroom please."

"Okay, when I come back I will help you do just that."

Sandy ran down the stairs shouting for Mildred. "She's hungry." David came out of the living room. "What did you say? She's hungry?

They all sat watching her eat. It was wonderful to see her eating. And she ate everything on her plate. Sandy turned to David.

"Wait till I tell Doctor Bain about this. This is what he wanted."

David wiped tears from his eyes.

"It is what I wanted too, just to see this."

Denise sat while Sandy brushed her hair back. "How would you like it?" Denise looked at David. "How would you like it?" David smiled.

"Anyway that makes you happy sweetheart but I like it pulled back to."

David smiled at Sandy and went out of the room laughing.

It was midday when the doctor rang the doorbell. Mildred quickly went to the door. "Oh doctor, wait till you see her. She is amazing to see."

"I can't wait." He quickly went up the stairs and into the room. They were laughing at a joke Sandy had told. He dropped his bag and went to her.

"Denise, is this the same girl I have been seeing?"

"I am such a girl you see."

"But, I have to check you to see if you are the one."

Sandy stood by him.

"Get me my bag please Sandy." He looked at Denise in a surprised way.

"Tell me how you are feeling right now, this very minute."

"I am very full of food." Everyone laughed.

"But how does your eye feel? Does it hurt you any?"

"My eye? Which one?" They laughed again. The doctor turned to them.

"Hush people, I have to know this, and it is not funny." He turned to her.

"Denise, I want to look at your eye okay. Now just lay down." He took the patch off and got his flashlight out. "Can you open your eye for me a little?"

She slowly began to open the eye. He looked very closely into it.

"Now, I want you to follow the light I will shine in your eye." The bright light passed across her face. "Tell me what you can see if anything."

"I see a bright spot, now it is gone."

"Good, that is all right Denise, I turned the light off." He looked again into her eye. The eye had a white milky film on the outer eye. He shined the light again moving it from side to side. "Can you follow the light with your eye?"

He moved it again. Her eye followed it from side to side. "Good girl."

He turned to Sandy. "Keep putting the drops in her eye and on the lid. Okay Denise, slowly close your eye and rest it." He stood shaking his head and turned to David. "I have never seen anything like this before."

"What do you mean?"

"The nerve around the eye has gotten stronger. This is unbelievable."

"That is good right?'

"Yes it is but how I cannot explain it. She must have an angel on her shoulder. That's all I can say. I'll have to check her tomorrow."

He kept shaking his head as he walked out the door. "Simply amazing."

Sandy went to her and looked at David. "He heard your prayer."

David followed him to the door.

"Will she be alright? Tell me the truth, will she?"

"Mr. Hunt, she is better than alright. See you tomorrow. Good night."

David had seen the doctor do everything, and he had been there to see it.

He leaned against the door and raised his head. "Thank you God."

A voice came to him. "She would like to see you now." Sandy was standing there with a smile of knowing all things.

A great tomorrow…

David sat in the office. Mildred passed by. "Mildred." He called out.

"Yes sir."

"Would you ask Sandy to come see me here, please?"

"Yes sir, right now." It only took a few minutes for Sandy to appear.

"You wanted to see me Mr. Hunt?"

"Yes, please come in and have a seat."

She sat down. "Is anything wrong sir?"

"On the contrary, in fact, everything has been going too well."

"I think that is a good thing, don't you?"

He sat back in the chair. "Tell me something. Are you a religious person?"

"I am very much so."

"You told me a passage from the bible the other day remember that?"

"Yes."

"Well I have one maybe you can help me with."

"I will try sir."

"The bible also says, 'Thou shall not kill' is that true? I'm talking about the man with the gun and about him about to shoot it."

"The Lord has said something else too. He said, "Protect my temple." Perhaps that is what you were doing. It may take violence to protect something or someone you love. I know you could have killed that man, but God gave you another answer and you followed that answer. I saw that in your eyes."

"And what did you see in Denise's face?"

"Fear, but not for herself, but for you. She loves you very much."

David looked at her for a long while and then spoke.

"Did the hospital send you here to help Denise? Or was it the doctor?"

"I ask to be here, to help in any way I could. I ask to help Denise and I was granted the permission to be here. I pray for her every day, every night."

"Maybe that's what I feel. I feel a spiritual feeling in this house.

A presence of you. A spiritual presence. Do you know what I mean?"

"I know God is everywhere. I believe that he has allowed me to be here."

"Getting back to the hospital, did you work in Denise's ward?"

"The hospital is a very large place. I have worked in many rooms and have been of help to many. Mr. Hunt, do you not wish me to be here?"

"It is a pleasure for you to be here. You have brought life back to Denise and also to me. In fact, I want you to stay with us always if you can get permission to do that from, well let's say from whom ever."

He watched her stand and go to the door. She turned to him.

"It is a greater power than I to answer your request." She turned and left.

He sat not knowing what to say. He just tapped his cane on the desk.

Denise sat up in bed with a tray of food before her.

"Would you want some of this great food?" Sandy just smiled.

"No thank you. Mildred made me a big plate earlier. May I tell you something about your husband?"

"I know he is wonderful to me. What you tell me?"

"Did you know he talks to God about you? He prays and asks God to guide him in all ways. He is a remarkable man and you make him very happy. He has many questions and many answers. You are lucky to have him."

"Why you tell me this?"

"Because I see things that I, too, think is wonderful. The way he looks at you, the way he holds your hand and touches you. You will see all this in time."

"I do love his touch, his eyes when he looks at me makes me feel safe."

Sandy looked at her watch. "It is getting late, eat up girl friend."

"You sound like Charlotte. She say girl friend too." Denise giggled.

"Yes she is something else alright. Finish up, I'll be right back."

It was ten o'clock as Sandy was putting drops in Denise's eye.

"Get a good night sleep now and things will be much better tomorrow."

"Can I go outside tomorrow? I wear sunglasses and patch."

"We will see how the weather is and the doctor will be here early too."

"I wish you were my doctor. You know everything to do for me."

"No I don't know everything, but I know someone that does. Good night."

David popped his head in the room. Denise was fast asleep. He went to her side and pulled the blanket up on her a little. Sandy stood at the door.

"It won't be long before you two will be traveling all over the world."

"I hope so, I mean I hope it won't be long before she can see with both eyes."

"She is doing better than the doctor expected. Say your payers tonight."

He turned to see her but she was gone. How does she do that he thought.

He did say his prayers that night.

"Dear Lord please hear me. Let her see again. Let her be strong in body and in mind. Lord, help me too. I need an answer from you. Can I have an arm? I want to hold her as never before. If not, I will understand, amen."

The day started off early as the doorbell rang. Mildred put the breakfast down and went to the door. "Good morning Ms. Charlotte."

"Hi Mildred, am I too early to see her?"

"No mam I was just taking breakfast to her."

"Let me do that for you."

"Thank you, I do have other things to do." Charlotte with brief case in one hand and the tray started up the stairs. She opened the door slowly.

Sandy had just finished brushing Denise's hair.

"Good morning ladies." With a smile she went to Denise.

"Look what I brought you, breakfast. Oh, you look beautiful today."

Denise was always glad to see Charlotte. "I feel that way too."

"Here, eat your breakfast while I fix your hair." Sandy looked at her.

"You don't like the way I brushed it?"

"Well you could have done a better job. Do it like this."

Sandy watched her.

"I really don't like it that way. It makes her look too old."

"Well I do. Why don't you go do something, somewhere?"

Denise spoke. "You are my best friends and you should not argue about my hair."

"You are right. Look what else I brought you." She took out a magazine.

"Oh good, "WOMEN SPEAK OUT" I love this book."

Sandy took it from her and tumbled through a few pages.

"Oh this is interesting. Says here, "Don't believe everything your friend tells you today." She smiled. Charlotte grabbed the magazine looking at it.

"It does not. You made that up." Sandy went to Denise with a kiss.

"I'll be back in a little while girlfriend." Charlotte watched her leave.

"She is not your girlfriend, I am."

Again Mildred went to the door. "Good morning Doctor Bain."

"Good morning, is breakfast ready? Is she up?"

"Yes she is and Sandy and Charlotte are with her sir."

"No breakfast, I was just kidding you. Coffee would be nice."

"I will bring it up to you sir." As he entered the room they were giggling.

"Good morning Denise, Charlotte I see you two are having fun."

"Yes we are. How do you like her hair doctor?"

"Myself, I like it down." Charlotte frowned.

"Okay, let's get to it. Are you alright today Denise?"

"Yes fine, thank you for asking." He laughed at her comment.

"That is what doctors say." He opened his bag and started checking her.

"Heart beat it good. Blood pressure normal. Let me look at your eye now."

As he took the patch off, she slowly opened her eyelid.

"Very good, your muscles are getting stronger, very good."

He took the flashlight out and turned it on. He waved it across her face and leaned in for a closer look. "Okay, follow the light." She did.

Charlotte looked over his shoulder. "What do you see doctor?"

"Please Charlotte, just stand back, okay."

"Okay, sorry." He leaned in again looked at the eye with the flashlight.

"Do you have any headaches today Denise?"

"None much, but I will ask you a question. Can I go outside today? It would be good to walk around some. Sandy could go with me and Charlotte too."

"We will see. Just want to look again. Move both of your eyes from side to side, slow now." He backed the light off as she moved both of her eyes.

"Very nice, your muscles are much stronger today. That is a good sign."

Charlotte sat pouting. Sandy stood at the Door. "Ha, ha, ha" She came in.

"Doctor Bain, is there anything I can do?"

"Yes Sandy you can."

"What sir?"

"You can take her for a walk." He turned to Denise. "But she must wear sunglasses and the patch always."

"Charlotte come too?"

He turned to Charlotte. "You want to walk with them? You can help Sandy." A smile came to her.

"I would love to walk with Denise if that is okay with Sandy."

Sandy nodded her head. "Only if I can brush her back down."

David came in the room. "I heard that. Can I go too?" The doctor gathered his things. "David, may I speak to you downstairs?"

They sat in the living room talking.

"David, it must be some kind of a miracle what has happened to her that I cannot explain. The milky film is almost gone and the muscles in the eyes are working together quicker than I expected them to. David, I thought it would be at the most a year but she is almost ready to see. I have talked to other doctors about this and they cannot explain it." Sandy stood at the door holding a small bag with some of Denise's things in it.

"She has eaten her breakfast, is wearing the patch and her sunglasses, and she is ready to go for the walk as you said she could do."

"Okay David, take the walk with them. I have real sick people to see."

The walking was fun for them all as they all held hands and sang songs and skipped along the path. Denise was all smiles as she and David stopped along the way to hug and kiss. Sandy turned to Charlotte.

"Having fun?"

"Yes thank you but I still like her hair the way I had it." She laughed.

And he said,

The evening was coming to an end of a great day. The sky was clear and the moon and stars were out in all their glory as the fireplace cast a warm light on them as they sat on the couch kissing and cuddling.

"Excuse me, sir I am going to bed now. Is there anything I can get for you?"

"For me nothing, David you want anything from Sandy?"

"Ah, yes. Sandy would you sit with us a while?"

"I would love to thank you." She came in and sat down.

"Sandy we both want to thank you for all you have done for us. You have brought a light to our home and into our lives, a light that has brought all three of us very close together. Can you explain that light to us?"

"The light was already here. Your love for each other was the light."

"But, there is a difference now."

"He has said, 'My children have been in darkness, but will see the light.'" She stood. "Is there anything else sir?"

He looked at Denise. "No, but tell whom ever, thank you from us."

"My wishes and prayers have been answered by being here. Good night." They watched as she seemed to float out of the room.

"I really love her don't you?"

"In a way yes I do. She is a strange and wonderful lady."

"Strange? How you say that? She is best for us ever."

"That you are right about."

Denise took his hand very excited. "Oh I have news from the doctor. He say, we should sleep together tonight."

David quickly looked at her.

"Really, well, let us get with it then." They headed up the stairs.

"Maybe we should have an elevator put in here, it would be faster going to the bedroom." She ran to the bed and jumped on it. "All night maybe."

The moonlight shined into the large bay window all night as they made love, all night.

"Hello, hello." Sandy came in their bedroom. David sat up.

"Oh I 'm sorry I didn't know you were here sir."

"What time is it?" She looked at her watch.

"It is right now, eight o'clock."

Denise lay with a pillow over her head. "Guess I over sleep."

Sandy put a breakfast tray on the table. "Good for you. You needed your rest. I'll be right back." She left the room.

"Honey, are you asleep?"

He got up and put his robe on.

Sandy was outside the door as he was about to go out.

"Mr. Hunt, I'm sorry about bothering your sleep."

"That's alright. It's Sunday and I sometimes sleep in anyway. Go on in."

As she went in, Denise yawned and sat up in bed.

"Good morning sleepy head. Your breakfast is ready."

"It is very early to eat."

"Did you get enough exercise yesterday?" Denise smiled.

"I got more last night." Sandy laughed.

"Oh you are a bad girl. I think I know what you mean."

"Let's put your drops in first then you can eat, okay."

Denise laid back down as Sandy removed the patch from her eye.

"Okay honey, slowly open your eye." She looked in the eye very closely.

"Your eye looks very good today. The redness of your eye lid is great."

She added the drops to the eye. "Now close your eye." Denise did.

Sandy made the sign over her heart. She touched the eye softly with her hand. She closed her eyes and said a quick prayer. She took her hand off of Denise's eye and stood looking at her.

"I think the doctor will be pleased when he sees you tomorrow."

"What you mean?"

"I was told that you will be alright now and your eye will be healed."

"I hope you are right. I am so tired of this patch."

"Tell you what. Leave the patch off today, the air will do it good."

"Really, can I do that?"

"Sure, but stay away from the window. No bright light."

"I will do as you say Sandy." Sandy put the tray on the big table.

"Why don't you eat here today?"

"No tray on my bed for me?"

"Let's try something different today. Sit at the table." Denise got out of the bed and went to the table and sat down. Sandy pulled a chair from the table and sat down looking as Denise started eating her breakfast.

"My, you are hungry." Denise looked at her and smiled.

"It is all my exercise I am getting, you know." Sandy smiled.

"I think so."

David came back into the bedroom carrying the newspaper. "Okay if I come in?"

"Sure."

He went to the table and sat down. "Sweetheart, you don't have the patch on, why?"

"Sandy said not to wear it today, so no patch."

He looked at Sandy. "Well if she said no patch, no patch. I think she has answers for you."

Sandy smiled at him. "I have answers from whom ever."

Monday was a beautiful day. They sat in the breakfast room watching the humming birds flutter their fast wings as they drank from the feeder.

"They are so fun to see and watch."

"Can you see them Denise?"

"Yes, with both eyes almost."

"You mean with your new eye?"

"It is a little blurry, but yes I see."

"Do you see any colors? Like the red feeder? Or can you see the birds?"

"No red feeder, but I see the flying birds. They are so cute."

Sandy came in. "What are you guys looking at?"

Denise pointed. "See the humming birds? Their wings are very fast."

"They sure are. How is your eye today? Can you see them okay?"

"Some. Come see my eye. You know best."

Sandy stood looking at her eye. "My, the stitch has already gone. That is wonderful Denise."

David spoke. "A gift from whom ever, huh."

She looked at him. "Yes it is and only one more gift to go sir."

As the doorbell rang, Mildred answered it.

"Good morning sir."

"Hi Mildred, Where is everybody?"

"In the breakfast room sir, shall I show you?"

"Thanks, I know where it is." He went to them.

"Hello, hello, hello everyone, how is my girl today?"

"We see the humming birds today." He looked out of the window.

"They are great aren't they? I feed them myself."

He went to her. "No patch."

"No patch today. Sandy said no patch so I no wear patch."

"Well she knows a lot of things." He looked into the eye. "This is truly amazing. The stitch is gone, no redness on the eyelid."

He looked closer at the eye. "Amazing, just unbelievable."

David spoke to him.

"I want to thank you for last night."

"Last night, what do you mean?"

"We sleep together. You said we could. Thank you very much."

"I never said that but you are welcome, I think."

David looked at Denise.

"You are a very bad girl. I should spank you." Denise giggled.

"Please if you want to. It was very nice don't you think?"

"Well come to think about it, maybe I should thank you."

Sandy stood up. "Too much personal talk for me, what do you think about her doctor?"

He looked at David then at Denise. "Just amazing, that is what I say."

The doctor and David sat in David's office. He took out some papers and handed them to David. He looked them over.

"Been thinking about you David so I called a friend of mine. He specializes in your condition. He can help you if you want."

"You mean my arm?"

"Yes. The prosthetic or it is called a Trans humeral prosthesis can be put on your arm with no problem. The myoelectric is one that works with electrodes by the use of your muscles in the upper arm. You can even have a hand that will open and close. These are light and very strong."

"A hand too? But they look so unreal."

"Not today. They are made of a fiber that looks just like your skin tone."

"I have thought about it. I'll give it some more thought."

"Good, and when you are ready I will set up an appointment with him."

"Doctor Bain, you are a good man and a true friend, thank you."

"Mr. Hunt, you are a great man, and I thank you, so does America.

Okay David, I have to go but I will tell you that I am so glad to see the progress of Denise. She is a very special woman."

"That she is doctor, that she is. You have a good day sir."

"You to, and think about it okay."

"I will."

David sat looking at the papers telling him he could have an arm again and even a hand. It had been many years since he could hold anything. He touched the stub of his arm. The gunfire of the German plane flashed through his mind. He could still feel the pain as his plane went down.

Sandy stood at the door of his office.

"A man needs both arms to hold the one he loves."

He looked up but she was not there. He went out on the patio and sat down thinking about her and the way she treated Denise. Who was she?

"Hi my husband, I look for you everywhere."

"Hi baby, glad you found me. Come here."

He stood as she came to him. He put his one arm around her. He thought about the talk he and Doctor Bain had talked about. He kissed her and held her with the one arm he had.

"What would you think about me if I had two arms to hold you?"

"I think your one arm holds me very well. Why you ask me that?"

"Oh no reason, just wondering how you would feel about it."

"I love you David. Two arms make me no difference as we are together."

"Man, am I lucky to have you."

She laughed and giggled. "Me too, I am the lucky person."

Can I now?

A week had passed. David, Doctor Bain, and another doctor were talking. The doctor stood by a large chart on his wall pointing at an arm.

"This is your arm now. This is the prosthetic arm I recommend for you."

"Will it slide off easily?"

"Off and on as you wish, it is made especially for your stub you have now. Don't worry about it falling off, that won't happen. You also have the option to have this hand. It opens and closes as you move the muscles in the arm."

"Doctor Bain, what do you think?"

"It will make you a new life. As you can see this arm will allow you to do much of the things you did before. It is a great idea for you I think."

David sat looking at the chart on the wall.

"Give me some more time to think about it. So much is going on right now with Denise I just need time to think."

"I understand Mr. Hunt. How long has it been without your arm?"

"Twelve, fifteen years, maybe, so long I forget. I want to forget I guess."

"That is understandable. I am sorry you lost it."

David stood with his cane in hand.

"Thank you doctor for your time in talking to me, I will consider it."

The doctor stood too. "Thanks Frank, you have been very helpful."

They stood outside the tall building. Doctor Bain extended his hand. "Oh sorry, forgot you don't have a hand. David, think about it. I do want to shake hands with you someday and I know you want to also."

"Yes I do doctor, yes I do."

"Okay my friend, go take care of Denise and you have a good day."

"I will. Oh, I want to ask you something, how long have you known Sandy? She is an angel and we love her, but I was just wondering."

"Funny you asked about her. Not long really. She just appeared in my office one day asking if she could help me with my patients. I said sure."

"And she has been with you ever since."

"Well to tell you the truth, I think Denise is the first patient she has had."

"Thanks, you have a good day too."

As David drove home all he could think of was Sandy. She knew how and when to say things. Did she want something? Was she real? Could she really be a.. no, impossible. He sat in his driveway still thinking about her. Strange things are possible guess I will never know this answer.

The day started off as any other day. Birds singing, airplanes in the sky, and people running around the in Big Apple of New York. It was about ten o'clock in the morning. Denise and Sandy were playing checkers when a car drove up in the driveway. Charlotte and a lady got out and went to the door and rang the bell.

"Good morning Ms. Charlotte."

"Hi Mildred, can we see Denise?"

"Of course, just go right on up."

"Thank you." Charlotte turned to her friend as they climbed the stairs.

"She will be so glad to meet you." Charlotte knocked on the door and they went in the room.

"Hi you two, I want you to meet my friend, Susan Frost." Denise waved.

"Hi Charlotte, Hi to you Ms. Frost, please come sit." They did.

"Denise, Susan is the editor of Women Speaks Out, the magazine you like."

"Oh yes, I read it all the time. It is a great book."

"Well thank you Denise, I'm glad you like and read it, and I have heard so much about you."

"You mean my eye?"

"No, about you, you're French, and about you coming to America. Charlotte has also told me about your husband too." Sandy went to the door.

"If you need me, I will be downstairs. Keep that patch on till the doctor comes. He will be here in about an hour."

"I will do as you ask Sandy." Denise waved as Sandy left.

"She is my friend and my nurse." Charlotte reached for the hairbrush.

"Can I fix your hair?"

"You no like?"

"Well actually, no. I like it my way."

"Charlotte tells me you want to write a book. Maybe I can help you get it published. The magazine also publishes books too."

"Yes, we talk about it but I am not ready to do it just yet."

"I understand but when you are ready we will all get together and talk then and I hope it will be very soon."

"Yes Denise, Susan thought you could start with her magazine first in a short story about you and your times in France."

"I would like that very much, merci. You are very pretty lady Susan."

"Merci, to you Denise."

"You smell very nice today Charlotte."

"I try to always, some days better than other days I guess."

Susan handed Denise the latest copy of the magazine.

"Read this and tell me what you think about it the next time we meet."

"Merci, I read it today soon, merci."

"Okay sweet thing, we will go now. You have a good day, bye."

Susan shook her hand and Charlotte kissed her goodbye.

"I do hope we will get together soon, and I hope you are well soon."

"Thank you, I will be good soon I know. Chow for now."

"Chow sweetheart, bye."

David came in the room carrying some papers.
"Hi baby."

"Hi to you my husband, did you see my company?"

"Yes, we met down stairs, nice lady."

"She want to write about me in her magazine and a book too."

"Well she knows a lot about publishing I'm sure." He looked at the papers.

"I have some news too. I may get an arm."

"You may what?"

"Yep, Doctor Bain and I saw a doctor friend of his and he showed me how I can get an arm."

"That is wonderful David. When and how?"

"I don't know when or how, I am still thinking about it, but you will be the first to know. Now, let's talk about you. How do you feel today?"

"My eye it feels good today. Doctor Bain, he comes soon to see me."

"I'm glad you feel good. I have some calls to make so I will be back soon."

"Tell Sandy to come. I will win her more games with checkers."

David cracked up laughing. "You do that sweetheart, you do that."

Mildred came in with a tray of lunch for her.

"Would you like to eat here or go outside on the patio to eat Mrs. Hunt?"

"You know, outside would be nice to get sun on me."

"Yes mam, when you are ready it will be there."

Doctor Bain put his bag down and sat looking at Denise.

"It is nice out here in the sun, you need some."

"Yes, my body cries for sun. As a girl in France, I would lay in the sun for hours feeling of the warm air on my body."

"You really do miss France don't you? I can see it in your face. Okay let's look at you. Oh, yes, the milky white film is almost gone. Very nice, I want to have more x-rays taken of your eye later today. David can bring you."

"As you say doctor, we will be at your office later today."

"Good, now don't stay out here too long. I know it is nice, but the sun is stronger than you might think, okay. See you later. Bye."

David sat in his office on the phone.

"That is incredible news. You said the stocks would go up. Yeah, you do that, the sooner the better. Call me if any changes, okay bye."

He leaned back in his chair looking out the bay window. "Great."

Sandy stood in the doorway. "Good news?" He turned.

"Yes, very good news. Stocks split again." He hit the desk with his cane.

"Love it when that happens."

"I am glad for you sir. Anything I can do for you?"

"No thanks. Oh, Denise wants to beat you some more at checkers."

She tittered and turned away. "I'll take of that sir."

It was two o'clock when David and Denise sat in the reception room of Doctor Bain's office. "He will see you now." They went in.

"Good, right on time. We will go in here for the x-rays. Just take a minute to do this and I will know more." Denise sat with a light in her eye as he adjusted the machine. "Now hold still." She heard the click of the machine.

"Two more and we will be finished." Again they sat waiting for him. Soon he called them in his office. "It always amazes me to see this." He pointed to the eye in the x-ray hanging on the lit wall. "See this?" He pointed with a stick. "This shows me of an implausible recovery. How it is done is truly unreal to me but here is proof of it. I would say that within a week, you should start seeing colors."

David stood and shouted. Denise snickered.

"Sandy told me this. She say, soon."

"Well she is right but it may take a little longer. You must be very careful what you do. You could strain the muscle or the nerve."

"I will see that she will not do that doctor."

"He takes very good care of me."

"I'm sure he does but you must get plenty of rest and no sun for a while."

"Can I do exercises? Maybe walk some?"

"If you walk at night only, you hear me only at night."

"Can we make love at night?"

He chuckled. "I think, yes."

"You hear David, at night we can."

"And let Sandy keep putting the drops in your eye to. Now go home and do as you do and I will see you two in a few days."

They left the office holding hands. As David opened the car door, Denise kissed him. "He is a very good doctor, you think?"

"I think, yes he is."

"And he say we could walk and make love at night too."

"He did at that sweetheart, he did at that."

Mildred greeted them at the door.

"What did the doctor say?" Denise squeezed David's hand.

"He say to do it at night."

"Do what?"

David just stood there and chuckled. "You really don't want to know."

"Is food ready? I am very hungry today."

"Yes mam, it is almost ready."

Charlotte drove up as they were going in the house and tooted.

"Hey wait for me." She ran to them.

"Tell me tell me, what did he say?"

Denise grabbed her hand excitedly. "You come, I tell you all things."

They all had finished dinner and were in the living room talking.

"David, do you mind if Denise and I have just a girl talk?"

"No not at all, got some papers to look over anyway." He got up and kissed Denise. "I'll be in my office if you need me." He left the room.

"How is your eye honey? Can you see any better?"

"Oh yes, the doctor's x-ray was very good he say."

"Great. What I wanted to talk to you about is birth control. You do know about that right? I know it is not my business but just checking."

"You talk about the pill? Yes I take care of that. I am not pregnant."

"Well that is a load off my mine. But you do want to have a family."

"Yes but there is time for that later. You want family?"

"Not any time soon." She snickered. "No love for me yet."

"Why you not in love? You are a beautiful woman."

"Guess I am not as lucky as you. See, love has come to me many times but never stays very long. A weekend, an overnight stand, a day, but you and David have a love that many of us will never have. An everlasting type."

"Yes we fell in love many years ago. I knew it the first kiss we had we would always kiss forever."

"A kiss forever, wow. That is a dream. Anyway, I just wanted to talk with you about things. I feel much better now."

"May I ask you something? You say, a weekend, a overnight, a day, why you do that? You no want to fall in love like we do?"

"I would love to but I am searching for mister right I guess. I have never had a kiss that last forever but one day, who knows."

"Charlotte you are my best friend and I hope you will find that kiss."

"Me too sweetheart, but I am very hard to get along with. I kind of like thing my way, like your hair. Can I brush it up my way for you?"

It is time you see…All things.

The week had gone by fast as Sandy stood by Doctor Bain's side.

"I have new eye drops to start giving her. These are to be given only once a day. They will take the redness out of the eye and it will clear up."

"Yes sir. You think it will take very long?"

"Why do you ask?"

"Sir, there are others that I should go to, others that I must help."

"Of course, I understand. I can get another nurse if you want to leave."

"You want to leave me? No you must not go from me, I need you Sandy."

"I will always be with you my sweet, in your heart, in your thoughts. I will always be by your side always."

Denise reached for her hand. "And David also?"

"And David also, I will watch over you both always."

Doctor Bain put his things in his bag looking at Denise.

"You can stop wearing the patch for a while. I'll see you in a few days if you need anything let Sandy know I will stay in touch with her. Bye."

Doctor Bain stopped by David's office on his way out.

"How is she doing doctor? Everything is okay?"

"Definitely, it has amazed me about her progress. She should be seeing colors clearly in a few days now."

"That's wonderful. And things and people and books."

"Yes and even you." He gave a belly laugh. "And even you clearly."

The news was ecstatic and emotionally exciting to hear. He sat thinking of all the things that now they could do together now. She would be able to see without the patch she hated to wear. They could go anywhere now without her being aware of her eye and people looking at her. With cane in hand he went to her.

"Honey I just heard the great news."

"What you hear?"

"Oh he didn't tell you, guess he wanted to tell you himself so I won't tell."

Sandy was sitting there. "Isn't it great news?"

"David, Sandy wants to leave us."

"No you can't do that Sandy. I thought we talked about that.'

"There are others that I must go to and help."

"Have I done or said something wrong? Don't you like us anymore? You want more money? What does it take to make you stay? Aren't you happy?"

"I am very happy to see two people in love, but I must go soon."

"I don't understand you Sandy. We have been a family for a long time now and all of a sudden you have to go. It's not right, you hear me, it's not right."

"Denise and you do not need me any longer."

"Need? That is bullshit. You don't know what we need. All you think about is what you need to do. Well if that is the way you feel, go find your need."

He turned and stormed out of the room. Denise started to cry.

"I have never seen him this way."

"I will talk to him again. I know his feeling right now, it will be alright."

Several days had passed. David sat in his office as Sandy knocked on the door. He looked up and saw her standing there.

"Aren't you gone yet? When are you leaving?"

She came to him. "You are a very kind man and a man of principal. A man that cares about people and you should understand that I to care about helping people. That is what I was sent here to do, care for Denise."

She leaned on the desk looking at him. "I see your love. I see your pain. I feel you resentment of me right now and I understand. How can I help this?"

"By not leaving Denise, she is weak and needs you. I need you."

"Do you need or do you want?"

He hit his cane on the desk. "Both damn it, both. We need and want you to stay with us."

"I, too, have needs and wants. I want to stay but I need to go. It is my calling from as we say, whom ever."

"Okay, okay, go but I want you to remember her as a woman you could have helped more if you would have stayed with her."

"I am only leaving her body, not her mind. I will always be there for her even if I have left her. She will always be in my mind, always, and if she would ever need me, I will be there. David, I will be there for you too. You and she will live in my heart forever." She went to him.

"This is for you. I believe it will bring you much happiness."

She put a box on his desk and turned to leave.

"What is this? A going away present?"

She smiled as she left the office. "Not a going away present just a gift from, whom ever."

David sat looking at the box on his desk. He turned the chair around looking out the bay window. Maybe he had been a little rough on her. She was a kind of a spiritual woman that he had not known before. He turned looking at the box. Slowly he opened the box.

"What is this? A pair of shoes? Why would she give me a pair of shoes?"

He took one out of the box and sat looking at it. "Nice gift." He bent and untied his shoe and took it off. He took the new shoe and put it on his foot.

"Nice fit." He took the other shoe and put it on his bad foot. A very strange feeling came over him. A feeling he had never felt before as he stood looking down at the shoes.

He reached for his cane and started walking around the desk. His bad foot began to feel stronger as he walked. "What the hell." He took a few more steps and put the cane on the desk. Slowly he walked around the room.

"Sandy, get in here." He walked to the door and shouted. "Sandy." For the first time in many years he was walking without the cane. Cautiously and slowly he walked to the bottom of the stairs and shouted again for her.

Sandy sat talking to Denise in French.

"IL est temps pour votre medicament."

"Are you putting the new drops in my eye?"

"Yes."

"Vous etes la meilleure infirmiere."

"Merci, I try to be the best nurse for you."

"Are you really going away? Will you be back to see me?"

"I am always here for you, in your mind I will stay, always."

"I vous aimerai toujours."

"I will always love you to Denise, toujours." She touched Denise's eye.

"Je dois y aller maintenant." She took her hand away from Denise's eye.

"I know you must go and mes yeux verront que vous allies."

"Yes, your eyes will see me go. I love you Denise very much." Sandy stood.

"IL appellee a moi maintenant. I must go." Denise started to cry again.

"Will you hug and kiss David for me? He is a wonderful man."

"Yes, I will hug and kiss him for you. I will love and miss you very much."

Sandy went to the door. "You will see all things in two days." She threw a kiss to Denise and she was gone. David opened the door and walked in.

"Where is she? I got to talk to her."

Denise went to him and hugged him and kissed him.

"She has gone. The kiss was from her."

"Gone where? She can't just leave like that."

"She said that he has called for her and she must go from us."

"But look what she has given me. She gave me my foot back."

"And she gave me my sight back so I can see you again with both eyes."

David slowly sank down in a chair. "But, now I can't thank her for this."

"She told me that you have blessed her in many ways. That just watching the way we love each other would always be in her mind."

"But it is not fair her leaving us this way. We needed her, she knew that."

"She also said, lui dire au revoir pour mo."

"What does that mean?

"Tell him good bye and I love him very much." David started to cry.

"And I loved her very much."

It was late at night as David stood looking out the window. He looked at Denise sleeping in their bed. He stood thinking about Sandy and the ways she had about her. Denise came and stood by his side and put her arms around him. They stood looking at the dark sky and the moon and stars.

A shooting star flew by high in the sky.

"You think that might be Sandy?"

"No honey, just a shooting star."

"It is not the same here without her."

"No it isn't. You should go back to bed and rest your eyes."

"She say I see all things in two days. You think I will?"

"If that is what she said, then it will be true."

Denise sat at her dresser looking into the large mirror at her eyes. The new eye had cleared of the milky film and the redness was almost gone. She leaned in closer looking at the eye. She could almost see herself.

"David, come quick, I can almost see me."

He got out of the bed and came to her. He leaned over her shoulder. "Can you see me?"

"You are very soft but I see an outline of your face."

"Great. I have to call Doctor Bain and tell him the news."

"This is Doctor Bain's office, please leave a message."

"This is David Hunt can you call me or come to the house? It is about her."

It was an hour later Doctor Bain rang the doorbell. David opened the door. "Is she alright? I came as quickly as I could."

"She is fine but I had to let you know. Come see her." They went in the bedroom and Doctor Bain sat down beside her at the dresser.

"Tell me what you see Denise."

"I see you almost but you are a bit out of focus."

"Okay that is all I wanted to hear. David, bring her to my office later today."

"Is the eye okay?"

"Yes, I think she is ready." Denise looked at him.

"I ready for what?"

"You are ready to see my child, ready to see."

"What does that mean, ready to see doctor?

"I want to test her eyes again with a reading chart and check both eyes."

"Then what doctor."

"Then we will know exactly what she needs to do."

It was later that day they entered Doctor Bain's office. The nurse called for them. "The doctor will see you now." They went in.

"Okay Denise, sit here on this stool and look straight ahead at that chart."

She looked at David and sat down. "It is okay honey."

"Now I want you to cover you right eye with this paper and read the first line for me. Tell me the letters that you see."

"The letters I cannot read."

"Why? Are you too far to see them?"

"No, they are not in French. They are in English." She giggled. "Just kidding with you Doctor Bain, okay I read." She started to read them.

"I see a 'B' and there is a 'Q' I think, and a not for sure, maybe a 'R' or is it another 'B' maybe?"

"Okay try your good eye. Cover your new eye and read the chart."

"A, C, U, S, R, what do that spell?

He cracked up laughing. "Good girl. Now come over here and sit down here. Put your head against the bar and open both eyes and tell me what you see."

"Things are not very clear."

"Okay, close your right eye and read the letters." She read then all.

"Good, now the other eye."

"The letters are again not too clear." He turned the lens. "Now?"

"Oh, I see letters almost." He moved the lens again. "Now?"

"S, I, D, E, O, B,"

"Again, read the next row of letters."

"U, C, R, A, N, I think, no it is a "M" am I do it right?"

"Yes, you do it right Denise, yes you do. Okay that is all I need to know."

She stood and went to David. He hugged her with a little kiss.

"You did good sweetheart. Now what doctor?"

"Now I will write a prescription for her glasses."

"Glasses, she needs glasses?"

"Yes, for a while. Her new eye is still weak and with glasses she will be able to see things much more clearly. It may take a year of so but she will be fine. There is an eye care center down the street that will fill the prescription."

David looked at the small paper and at Denise.

"Thank you Doctor Bain, thank you very much." Denise turned to him.

"Medecin vous etes un home bon. Merci."

"What does that mean?"

"I think she said that you are a great doctor and thank you."

"Well merci to you Denise. I know that word."

Denise went and hugged and kissed him. "You are a great man."

The eye doctor handed her the glasses. "Try these on." She closed her eyes and put the glasses on. "Okay honey, open your eyes." Slowly she opened her eyes and shouted. "David, I can see you clearly now." He grabbed her with a big kiss. She looked into the mirror on the counter.

"I see me too. Oh David it has been so very long." She had tears in her eyes.

"Yes sweetheart but it has come true. Let me see your beautiful blue eyes."

She turned to him. "See me and my blue eyes, what you think?"

"Oh those candy blue eyes looking back at me is my dream, and the glasses are very pretty on you. What do you want to go see first?"

"You know what I want to see first? That beautiful hotel high in the mountains where we stay one time, remember?"

"Yes, I remember and we will go there."

"Wait till Charlotte see me and I will see her."

"You can call her when we get home. She will want to see her new friend."

"I wish Sandy could see me and I could see her now."

"Maybe she does see you now. Come on, let's go home."

Charlotte ran up the stairs of the house and rang the doorbell.

Mildred answered it. "Oh Ms. Charlotte, wait till she sees you."

"Oh I am so happy, where is she?"

"They are sitting out on the patio mam." Charlotte ran to them calling.

"Denise, David, where are you two?"

"We here Charlotte." Denise and Charlotte stood hugging.

"Step back and let me look at you. Wow, you are gorgeous."

"I feel pretty to. Now I see you with both my eyes."

"And I love those glasses you have."

"Yes David say he can see my blue eyes looking at him."

"David, what do you think about your new girl now?"

"I have waited a long time to see her looking like this."

"We are going to the mountain hotel and see everything again."

"Can you see things good with the glasses?"

"Oh yes but some things I need what you say, bio glasses?"

"Close, they are called, bifocal glasses." She laughed.

"I, too, must wear them to see some things. You get use to them.

Say, why don't the three of us go have lunch?"

"Excellent idea, Denise are you hungry?"

David snickered. "She is always hungry."

"I'll buy my treat." Denise and Charlotte hugged as they went to the car.

"Oh I have a new copy of your favorite magazine for you."

David looked at Charlotte. "Oh that's just what she needs, that magazine."

The night was made for passion. Denise sat on top straddling David as she breathed heavily. "Wow, that was incredible." He had his hands around her large breast as he massaged her nipples and they slid between his fingers.

"Wow is putting it without words." She giggled as always.

"You can do it again maybe?"

He laughed. "Maybe in about ten minutes."

"We can do it doggie kind as you like that. I like that to."

There was a knock on the door. "Mr. Hunt, I will be leaving now."

"Okay Mildred, have a good weekend."

"You and Mrs. Hunt do the same." Denise looked at him.

"Now, we can do it again now?"

"I think now we can do it again." The bed shook for an hour more.

David lifted the trunk of the car and put bags in it. He went back in the house calling. "Are you coming or not, come on." She came with two more bags. "You no leave without me." She handed him the bags.

"I must take these."

"Honey, we are just going for the weekend you know."

"I know but I need my things." She followed him to the car.

"Why you take your cane? Your leg hurt you?"

"No, just want to make sure it doesn't, ready?"

"I am, are you?" She giggled again. "A quickie maybe."

"You read too much, get in."

It was a long beautiful ride as the wind blew Denise's long brown hair. David turned the radio station to another station. He sat enjoying the music as he watched her wave at cars passing by. "They can't see you."

"I know but it is fun to wave. I remember as a child my mother and father would take trips and I sat in the back seat and would wave at all cars."

"That is a good times you must have had."

"Oh yes it was good times. I wish I still had pictures of them."

"Why don't you?"

She thought of the war and the bombs dropping.

"They were destroyed long time ago."

David pulled the car to a stop. "Lunch time, you hungry? Guess that is a dumb question."

"Oh same place we eat before."

"Yes, this is the halfway point."

"Maybe we see the fat man as before. He rude man, remember?"

"I remember, come on I am hungry too."

"Sign say, 'Welcome' and I welcome them to join us."

The hotel was as great looking as before. Denise quickly opened the car door and stood looking at the tall building. The attendant came quickly to the car. "Hi sir, I remember you two people, Mr. Hunt right?"

"You are right, very good. Could you…"

"Wash and gas it. I remember. Yes sir."

"David look, I not see this before. Could it be new?"

"No honey, it is your glasses. You will see lots more things now."

As they entered the hotel, the manager quickly came to them.

"Mr. and Mrs. Hunt, it pleases me to see you both again. I hope your trip here was enjoyable. Your room is ready for you, and thank you for coming."

"And merci to you sir."

"Ah, Mrs. Hunt." He kissed her hand.

"You are as beautiful as always. There is something different about you."

"It is my eye. I can see you and all things now. See my glasses?"

"Very becoming to you Mrs. Hunt, very nice." He called for the bellboy.

"Get their bag and take them to room twelve twenty please."

"Right away sir."

"Would you care for a cocktail before you go to your room sir?"

"What do you think honey? Your favorite drink maybe."

"That would be very nice."

The manager took them to the lounge. "Enjoy sir, here is your key. If you need anything please call me."

Denise sat looking around the large room.

"It is wonderful to see all things David."

"Here, let me have your glasses, there is something on them."

He wiped them off and handed them back to her. She put them on again.

"Wow, I can see very clear now. You are so good to me."

"That's just the start. Tonight we will dance, drink and be merry."

"Be merry? You silly man, we are married."

"No I mean, you're right sweetheart we are married." He smiled at her.

"May I get you something from the bar sir?"

"Yes please, a bottle of your best wine, is that alright with you honey?"

"Yes, and two glasses please."

David cracked up laughing. "I think he knew that sweet."

"One never knows. I ask for wine one time and there was no glass."

"You're right, why didn't I think of that." Again he laughed.

"It is so good to see your face with a laugh on it."

"I can't help it. Every time I look at you I am very happy."

"I love you so very much David, so very, very, much."

"And you are my best girl ever and I love you very, very, much."

"You want a quickie?" She laughed. "Just kidding with you."

They danced slowly to the romantic music as David held her tightly. Denise gazed into his eyes. "This is a wonderful moment."

"Yes it is and maybe next year I will have two arms to hold you with."

"I don't need two arms to hold me just two lips to kiss me."

"Always sweetheart, I will kiss you always till death do us part."

"And you will be my last breath my husband." The music ended.

"Let's go sit at our table under the moon and stars and talk."

The candle seemed to wave at them as they sat. A shooting star shot through the sky. "You see that David, a star just for us. Do you think?"

"You never know, it might have been."

"I miss her so much."

"Me to, but life must go on without her."

"You think we will ever see her again?"

"I doubt it, but she said she would watch over you, and I will too."

The waiter came with their menu and handed it to them. "Drinks sir?"

"Yes please, a bottle of good wine." He looked at Denise.

"And two glasses." Denise grabbed his hand and giggled.

"Can you read the menu alright?"

"Oh yes, I want all things." He laughed and squeezed her hand.

"You have the most beautiful eyes. I love to look at you. Your candy blue eyes looking back at me, reminds me of a girl long ago."

"It is thanks to you that I can see again. If it were not for you I would still be lost in a world without you. You make my dream come true in many ways."

The waiter came back and opened the bottle of wine for them. He poured their glasses and stood. "Anything else sir? Are you ready to order?"

"Not just yet thank you."

"When you are ready, my name is Paul sir."

"Merci Paul."

"Merci, to you mam. Enjoy your wine and the night."

"Parlez vous Francais?"

"Some, I lived in Paris for a while."

"That is where I am from."

"If you wish anything more, I will be close by to assist you." He went away.

"He is a very nice waiter you think."

"Very nice." David held his glass up. "A toast to us, and the night."

"And may they be as they are tonight my husband, always."

The music started playing again.

"Would you like to dance again?"

"Not now David. Could we take a walk by the water's edge as we did before there is something I would like to talk to you about."

The water lapped against the shore as they walked along in the bright moonlight. Denise pointed to a large group of rocks by the water's edge.

"There, can we sit there and talk?"

"Sure that looks like a nice spot." As they sat there, Denise looked troubled.

"Is there something wrong honey?"

"I have something on my mind that bothers me."

"And what may that be?"

She turned to him and held his hand. "David, I would like very much to go back to France. Not for a long while but just for a few days."

"Well, we can do that. Is there any reason to go back there?"

"Yes. Ever since I lost my eye and got this scar on my neck I feel that I need, how you say, closure. I lost a big part of me there."

"Denise, look at me. I did too. I gave a big part of me to France."

"Yes you did and I am proud of you. So is France."

"What is it there that you are looking for?"

She sat very quietly thinking. "Maybe to see the past with both eyes open, and to look for the future."

"Sweetheart we are in the future. There is so much ahead of us."

"David, I hear bombs falling. I see in my mind people that lay dead in the streets. I feel that building falling on me. Can you not understand?"

"Yes I can and I feel the same way, but that is over with sweetheart."

"Not for me David, not for me it is not over."

"Well I guess there is only one thing to do. We will go back to Paris France and put a lot of pieces back together for you and maybe me too."

"David, I will never ask for anything of you ever again."

"Honey, you just keep asking of me anything your heart desires and you may have all your wishes come true. Don't you know that I love you?"

"I know you do. You have given me this eye that now I can see, and a home here in America that I can call home, and most of all, your love."

"Well say no more. Let us make plans and we will go to France."

"You see, as we talk you give of your heart to me."

"Well for now, let's go eat. I know you can do that." He laughed. "Ready."

"I will be there before you."

She started running down the shore. She stopped and held out her hand.

"You are well ahead of me in mind and in spirit, slow person."

He cracked up laughing at her. "It is slow poke silly woman."

"Oh, you want to poke me?"

"Yep, tonight I will poke you."

"Is that your promise?"

"It is not only a promise but a guarantee."

She giggled and threw sand at him. "Now I am hungry kind sir."

Going back home.

The trip to the mountains was very refreshing for both of them as they sat having their morning coffee on the patio.

"It is going to be a great day, just look at that sun coming up."

"Not as lovely as in the mountains but you right, it is very pretty."

"So my lovely wife, have you thought about when you want to leave?"

Robert Cory Phillips

"Maybe soon the better. Like four days maybe. Is that good for you?"

"Four days would be great, that will give me time to make plans."

"I will call Charlotte and tell her. She will be excited for us going."

"I have some calls to make myself so I'll see you later. Love you."

He got up and walked away with his cane.

"Love you." She whispered.

Charlotte stood ranging the doorbell. "Good morning Ms. Charlotte."

"Hi Mildred, you look nice today."

"Thank you, I am going to visit my daughter today. She lives up state."

"That's nice. So where is she? She wanted me to come over here."

"I think she is outside on the patio. I will show you."

"That's alright, I know where that is."

She patted her hair down, put her bag down and went to find her.

"Hey girlfriend what you doing out here?"

"Hi you girlfriend, I sit here thinking." Charlotte sat down."

"Oh yeah, what are you thinking about?"

"I have news for you. We are going to Paris France."

"You are what? When are you going? Why?"

"When is in four days why is long story."

"I have time, tell me."

"It is I am homesick to see there and want to see things there with both eyes as I did long ago. It was so beautiful then."

"Well I understand homesick but I'm sure things have changed a lot there."

"David say, change is a part of life.'

"And change is a good thing to. It gives you another outlook on life."

"I just want to see French people, things there, French food, you know."

"So how was the trip to the mountains?"

"It was a wonderful time there. David is so good to take me there."

"Yeah, I like him too. Do your glasses still fit you okay?"

"Oh yes, I see the hotel very well and the mountains too."

"Your hair is a mass of string. Let me brush it for you."

"Okay, then will you help me make plans to go to Paris?"

They sat for hours making a plan. Charlotte was writing down things that she should take to Paris France.

"And don't forget your tampons." Denise giggled.

"I did forget them one time, it was very embarrassing to me."

"Well you never know when mother nature calls."

"Mother nature? I know not about this."

Charlotte laughed. "You will learn honey, you will learn about her."

Charlotte handed her the list and sat drinking her coffee.

David was talking on the phone. "Hi Ann, David Hunt here."

"Mr. Hunt, it is good to hear from you. How is married life?"

"Could not be better. Say, can you book us on French Air Lines for a six day trip? And a room at the Hilton Hotel there in Paris France?"

"I would be glad to sir. Would you like a car too?"

"No, the hotel is close to things we want to see and we can get a cab if we need to go someplace. Oh have the hotel have lots of flowers in the room."

"Got it. When do you want to leave New York?"

"Well today is Monday so how about Sunday."

"I will have your tickets ready for you and Mrs. Hunt to pick them up at J.F.K. Sunday morning. You do have your passports?"

"Good catch, I forgot about that, thanks."

"Okay Mr. Hunt, you and Mrs. Hunt have a great time there. It is a very good time to go there. The American dollar is up there."

"That's always good to hear. Thanks for everything, bye."

He went calling for Denise.

"Out here with Charlotte." He went and handed a paper to Denise.

"I got it together. We can leave this coming Sunday morning for Paris."

"Let me see that." Charlotte took the paper.

"Okay, J.F.K., tickets okay, depart time okay, hotel, no car okay, looks okay to me. Oh, I forgot to put passport on that list, you do have one?"

"Oh yes I do, two of them. A French one and an American one. Now I marry David, I can go anyplace I choose."

"Okay, I'll tell what I will do for you two. I'll pick you up early Sunday morning and take you to J.F.K. airport, how's that David?"

"Great, save us cab fare, thank you Charlotte. I knew you were good for something, just kidding with you."

"You better be just kidding. I sleep in on Sunday mornings." He snickered.

"How do you like the way I did her hair?"

"Well its nice, but..."

"No buts David, I like it this way and you need a haircut my friend."

A few days had passed as David stood looking in the mirror.

"Honey, I'll be back in a while. I'm going to get a haircut."

"She get to you the other day?" She giggled as she always did.

"No, just want to look good for the trip."

"Just one more day, we leave."

"Yep, tomorrow morning, better start packing things."

She came out of the shower carrying her robe. He looked at her.

"Wow, what a body you have, maybe I will go later to get a haircut."

She turned around and around modeling for him.

"You like maybe a quickie?"

"I'm beginning to like that word." She went to the bed and lay down.

"Come to me my handsome husband." He quickly did.

Sunday morning came early as David stood outside the house on the front porch beside six pieces of luggage. He puffed on his cigar and blew smoke in the air. Everything was ready to go except Denise. He shouted for her. "Denise, you want to go or not? She will be here any minute now."

Denise carried two more bags to the porch and put them down.

"You no shout at me, of course I want to go but bags are heavy."

"I'm sorry sweet, but a plane will not wait for us to get on it."

Charlotte drove up honking the horn "Wow, look at all the baggage."

"Yeah you and your list couldn't you make it a little shorter?"

She opened the trunk of the car and smiled.

"Got a haircut I see. Now you look much better, but go comb it."

"I like it this way Charlotte."

"Wow, grumpy in the morning I see. I'll help you with the luggage."

"Hi Charlotte, am I pretty?"

"Honey you always look pretty. I'll fix your hair before you leave."

"Okay Denise, you sit in front with her and I will sit in back and hold two of these bags you don't need."

"Isn't he nice to sit in the back seat?" She laughed out loud.

"Did you pack your fiber laxative David?"

"As a matter of fact, I did smart ass."

"He did I saw him do it, but you know, it do not taste good I try it."

"I know, I hate the stuff to. Okay guys, say bye to your house for a while."

"Bye big house. Oh David, you take Loaner to doggie place?"

"Yes I did, last night. Okay Charlotte, drive."

"Who do you think I am, Miss Daisy?"

"No, Miss Daisy is pretty but you will do, now drive please."

"Okay, you said please. And we are off, that includes you too David."

The freeway and streets were clear for a Sunday morning as they rode along. "You have your sunglasses don't you Denise?"

"Yes, I have three pair for me to wear different days."

"Oh David, when will you coming back?"

"I think we leave there on a Friday night and be here Saturday late night."

"Well, call me when you are leaving and I will pick you two up here."

"That's very nice of you Charlotte. I take back all the bad things I said about you except about my hair cut."

"Can't you take a joke? I think your hair looks as good as possible."

"What does that mean? I combed it like you said." Denise turned and looked at him. "It sticks up in the back a little."

"Oh you two hush. Well I like your hair down, not up like Charlotte put it."

Charlotte pulled up in front of the French Air gate entrance.

An airline attention came to the car as Charlotte opened the trunk of the car and stood counting the bags. "They are all here."

"I will take care of all your baggage mam. You are going to France?"

"No, they are." David put two more bags on the cart.

"Oh you are Mr. and Mrs. Hunt. Your tickets are inside waiting for you."

"Thank you."

"Here are your baggage tickets sir." David handed him a large bill.

"Merci sir, merci beaucoup."

"Okay you two, have a wonderful time there. Wish I were going too."

She went to Denise with a big hug. "I sure will miss you honey."

"I will miss you to but I will think of you every day."

She hugged David.

"Take care of her and take care of yourself too my friend."

She turned to Denise. "I got you something to read on your trip."

She handed her a magazine. "Oh goodie, look David, Women Speak Out."

"Oh great, just what you needed. Thanks Charlotte."

"You are welcome David, I thought you would like that."

The attendant came to David and handed him their boarding tickets.

"Your bags are on the plane and you will be leaving in about twenty five minutes sir, Would there be anything else sir?"

"Yes, could you ask this lady to leave please" He smiled at Charlotte.

A cab pulled up behind Charlotte's car and honked his horn.

"Guess I better leave now." She hugged both of them. "Call me."

The driver honked his horn several more times. Charlotte looked at him.

"Keep your shirt on feller." He honked again. She went to her car and sat there. She put her lipstick on and smiled at him. He honked again. She went to him. "What's your problem you jerk?" She gave him the finger.

They sat in the first class seats talking about this and that. An airline stewardess came to them. "Merci for flying with France Airlines."

"Oh, parlez vous francis?"

"Oui, I am French. How may I help you or get you something?"

"Yes, deux verres de champagne s'il vous plait."

"Very well, I shall return shortly."

"What did you say to her?"

"I ask for two glasses of champagne, that is good right."

"Oh yeah, perfect." David pulled out a book from his pocket.

"What you have there?"

He laughed. "Bought this book, English to French. Now I will be able to understand."

"Okay, what is this? Tellement je taime."

Wait, let me look it up. "How do you spell that?"

She laughed so hard. "I love you so much."

The lady came back with the champagne. "Here are your champagne and two glasses as you wished."

David quickly turned the page in his book. "Merci beaucoup."

"You are welcome sir, I will be with you always." She went away.

"Did you hear what she said? Sandy always said that."

"Yes she did, but for now, a toast to France and to you and I."

Their glasses touched and they drank. David sat looking out the window at the clear blue sky. I will be with you always kept going through his mind.

His foot and leg had gotten stronger almost every day. He looked at his cane and at Denise as she sat with her glasses on reading the magazine.

"David, I have joke for you."

"Okay, what is it?"

"Knock knock."

"Who's there?"

"Knock knock."

"Who's there?"

"Knock knock."

"Who is there?"

"Knock knock."

"Okay, I give up. What's the joke?"

"Nothing, I just like to say knock knock."

"You are a very silly woman, did you know that?"

"Knock knock." He hit her with his book. The lady came back to them.

"It is lunch time if you desire anything."

"Oh, can I have one of the small bottles of brandy, peanuts, a sandwich and more champagne please?"

"Of course and for you sir." David kept looking at her.

"Nothing thanks."

The flight was going well. People on the flight were playing games and just having fun. Denise was asleep and resting her head on David.

The airline stewardess came to him again.

"Sir, I have a pillow for her. I also have a pillow for your leg and foot."

"How did you know that I needed it? I do but how did you know?"

"Well sir, I saw your beautiful cane you have there and I am here to help you anyway I can. I will be with you always."

"What did you say?"

"I said I will be with you all the way to Paris sir."

"No, you said, "I will be with you always.""

"I'm sorry sir, you must have misunderstood me."

He looked puzzled. "I guess I did, sorry." He put a pillow under Denise's head and under his leg.

"Guess I did."

It was well into the flight and the moon was beginning to shine. He sat looking at the night and all the stars. He could almost touch them.

"Are we there yet?" Denise stirred and adjusted in her seat.

"No sweet, not yet but soon now." She went back into a slumber state.

David looked at his watch and laid his head on her and went to sleep.

The voice came over the speaker. "This is the captain speaking."

Denise shook David. He sat up and looked at his watch.

"We will be arriving in Paris France in forty minutes. Just want to thank you for flying Air France Airlines. We hope you have enjoyed your flight."

"Boy was that a fast three hours. How do you feel sweetheart?"

"I am very excited." The airline stewardess came to them.

"You should start getting your things together, we will be in Paris soon."

She took the pillows. "Would you like a drink from the bar?"

"Sure, a couple of bottles of water would be nice."

"I will get that now sir. Mrs. Hunt, would you like anything?"

"Yes, three more hours of sleep please." She laughed.

"I am just kidding with you."

"What time do you have?"

"I not sure we in another time zone now."

"Oh that's right, forgot about that." He looked out of the window.

"Look Denise, you can see the lights of Paris shinning."

"It is an amazing sight to see Paris from here in the sky."

The captain came back on. "We will be touching down in twelve minutes."

The lady came to them. "Buckle your lap belts now, it is that time."

The sound of the big jets engines roared loudly. They felt the plane going down and heard the tires hit the runway. "David, we are here."

And they were. The airline waitress came to them smiling.

"I hope your stay here in Paris France will be as you expect it to be."

"Merci." David gave her a hundred dollar bill. "You made it perfect."

"Oh merci beaucoup, Mrs. Hunt may I say to you, vous etes si belle."

"Merci, I feel beautiful."

"If you would like, you follow me and you can get off the plane first."

David looked into the coach area. People were standing up ready to get off.

"That would be very nice, we will follow you."

They walked off the plane into the huge airport of Paris France.

A driver dressed in a black suit held a sign with their name on it.

"David, how they know we are coming here?"

"The ticket agency told them to look for us. Come on." Denise stood looking at the tall buildings sky light. What a big place. I have never been here before."

"It is big. Hi, we are the Hunts."

"Glad to meet you sir, mam. Your baggage tickets please and I will take care of them for you and have them sent to the hotel."

"Good man. Where is the car? We are very tired, jet lag you know."

"Please follow me sir and we will be there very soon."

The big black limousine sat waiting for them. Quickly the driver opened the back door for them. Denise sat looking at the television set, the wet bar, and the large leather seat. "This is what we need David."

"Think so? Okay we will get one."

"And a driver person to. I cannot drive this big car."

He cracked up. "I cannot drive this big car too." He leaned to the driver. "How far from the hotel to the French Embassy would you say?"

"Maybe one or two miles sir, you wish to go there?"

"No we will go there another day."

"That is where your father worked is it not."

"Yes, I use to go there with him sometimes."

"I remember he was an important man. I remember your mother too."

"Yep, two great people and they loved you, remember?"

"I do remember both of them well. We had dinner together many times. At their house and at the restaurant, remember that time."

"Yeah, that was the night I ask you to marry me sometime."

"And I said, sometime I will." They held hands and laughed and laughed.

"Now look at us, married and back in Paris France."

"Je t'aime tellement."

"Oh no, I left my French book on the plane. Tell me what that means."

"I say, I love you so much."

The Hilton Hotel, a majestic building, one of the tallest structures in Paris, France with its many arms reaching to the sky. David stood looking out over the cascade of many buildings. He remembered when he had joined the French Air Force. A time in his life that changed him forever. He thought about all the great times with the other pilots and the not such good times.

Yes, Paris was the place where me and Denise had met and fallen in love.

A beautiful French girl and an American boy, who would ever have thought that they would have made it. Now as he looked at her there in the bed sleeping, he was proud of this French girl. The girl that had given so much for her country and to him. He looked at the ring on his finger with a smile that told it all.

Denise stirred in the bed and reached for him. He was not there.

"David, where are you?" She sat up and looked around.

He came to her. "Right here sweet."

"What time is it?" He looked at the clock on the table.

"Ten after twelve. You have been asleep for about ten hours."

"And you, you sleep good?"

"Very well. That flight took a lot out of us. Are you hungry?"

"I think as you say, a cow I can eat."

He laughed. "Actually, it is I could eat a horse."

"Oh, you are hungry too."

Again he laughed. "Would you like room service or would you like to go downstairs to eat?"

"I like to go down to eat food."

"Then down it is. Take your shower, put your pretty dress on and we go eat a cow." He laughed, she giggled.

It was almost two o'clock Paris time. They had finished their late breakfast and were standing in the great lobby of the hotel.

"That was very good no."

"That was very good yes. What would you like to do today?"

"Can we walk the streets, see the people and the café and maybe shop?"

"Yep, and shop for things for you and maybe something for me to."

"And for you to oh, did I tell you something? I love you today."

"And did I tell you that I love you every day."

The hotel manager came with flowers for Denise.

"Bien venue a Paris. For you Mrs. Hunt."

"Merci beaucoup. They are lovely, you think so David?"

"Yes very lovely. Read the card, see who sent them to you."

"It say here, juste pour vous, tellement je t'aime, David."

She hugged and kissed him. "I love you to my husband."

"Enjoy your stay with us Mr. and Mrs. Hunt."

The streets were filled with music, French people and tourist as they step from the hotel. "Can you feel the pleasure here David? Can you?"

"Yes I do, just look at all the people. I forgot how great it is here."

"Ah, Paris the most romantic city in the world David."

"Shall we walk?"

"J'ai rate France."

"Yes, la France est belle."

"Oh you speak French now." He took a French book from his pocket.

"Bought this at the gift shop. Now I am French too." She giggled as always.

"Let us go this way."

Vendors held things out for them to see and buy. People in the sidewalk café sat drinking wine. French flags blew in the air.

"Oh David look." A sign high on a building read, "Parfum de la lov."

"Oh, I must go there, come with me."

They could smell the perfume as they entered the shop. Denise quickly went to each counter looking and smelling of all the different kinds. She sprayed herself with one of them.

"Smell me." David put down a small bottle he was holding.

"Very nice, try this one." She held out her arm. "Spray here."

"Oh, so that's where you put it on."

"No silly man, this is where you sample it. You wear it behind the ear."

"I see now, that is why your neck always smells so good."

"Oui."

David took out his book. "Is that, we? or wee?"

She wandered around the shop and finally went to the shop owner.

"I take these three bottles please. One for Charlotte okay."

"A very good choice. I have a special one for you over here."

She followed him to another counter. He handed her a small spray bottle.

"It is with love that I give to you."

"Oh merci beaucoup, I love the smell of this, so much it is me, merci."

They stood outside of the shop. "Okay, where to now?"

"What time do your watch say?"

"It is now, half passed five. Why do you ask?"

"Maybe we go back to the hotel, I am still tired some, and you walk slowly with your cane. Do your foot and leg bother you?"

"Not really, but I could use the rest."

"Good, we go back to hotel, have a good dinner, and sleep early tonight."

"Sounds like a great idea." She wrapped her arm around his as they walked.

"Maybe if you not too tired, we make love tonight." He smiled.

"Maybe a quickie." She giggled with her great smile.

"And in the morning we do a long love making."

The day had come to an end and the city lights lit up the sky as never before. Denise sat looking at all the pictures that David had taken during the day. The perfume shop, the café where they had eaten, the vendors, the flag of France and the hotel where they were staying. She smiled at a picture of them overlooking the water falling in the mountain. She turned and watched as David lay asleep. All she thought of was how wonderful he was. He had given so much to her and to France. His arm, his leg and foot but even after all that she knew that he still loved France and the French people. It was not long after that she lay beside his sound asleep.

The morning sunlight came in the large window of their room and cast its light across their bed. David sat on the edge of the bed rubbing his eyes. He turned to see Denise sleeping with her long brown hair falling on the pillow. He lay back down looking at the sun as it fell on his cane. It seemed to have a glow about it. The cane seemed to be telling him that he would not need it very much longer. The longer he looked at it he could hear Sandy telling him, "I will see you again" but in his mind he knew that it would not happen. Denise opened her eyes with a soft little gentle smile.

"I see you." He turned to her.

"I see you too." He held her face in his hand and kissed her.

"How do you feel after a good night's sleep?" She stretched her arms.

"It is amazing to wake up after so long sleeping and feel this good."

"It is going to be an amazing day too."

"I look at the pictures last night and thought of all the new things here."

"Yep, Paris has changed since we were here last time."

"I think it is a good thing to see again these changes."

"And I have seen a change in you since we have been here."

"Is that not a good thing?"

"It is a wonderful thing. You are more alive and more beautiful."

They hugged and kissed for a very long time.

"Oh I feel something." She moved her hand under the sheets. "For me?"

"Well, you said we should make love for a long time this morning."

"That I did." She threw the sheet away and started kissing his body all over.

It was some two hours that they lay there cuddling and having fun.

David looked at the clock on the nightstand then pinched her nose. "The day is going fast. What would you like to do today? I have three things you might like. One, we can take a good boat ride all around Paris. Two, we can take the tour bus all around Paris and see everything or, three, we can stay in and make love all day and then dance the night away."

"David, there is one thing I would love to do."

"And what is that sweetheart?"

"I would love to see the house that I grew up in."

"You mean that big white house with the broken down wooden fence?"

"Yes I have a picture it in my mind for a long time."

"Then that is what we will do today."

"Thank you David, it will mean so much to me to see it again."

They stood in front of the hotel looking at the line of cabs waiting.

"May I get you a cab sir?"

"Yes please." The attendant called for the first cab in line. He opened the door of the cab for them. "Do you speak French sir?" They got in the cab.

"No, but she does, merci."

"Where may I take you to?"

The ride through the city was exciting to see. It was not too long before the cab turned off the main road on to a dirt road. Denise started looking for her house she had lived in long ago. "There, there it is David."

"Just pull off the road and stop by that fence there."

From a distance, Denise sat looking. A large sign was in the yard. They got out of the cab. "Wait here for us please." They stood by the fence looking at the house and the big yard. There were children playing in the yard. She looked at the sign again. "Val Jean's Children's Home" she read it. They stood watching the children playing jump rope, playing ball, running after each other and a tear came to her eyes. "David what is this?"

"It looks like a home for children, isn't it wonderful to see this?"

"But I thought it was a hospital. That is what it was."

"One of the many changes of Paris I guess but look at the kids playing there. You made a home for them, you gave them shelter, food, clothes and they look very happy to me." An older lady came out of the house. She stood as a small boy and a girl ran to her. She hugged them and seemed to look at the fence where Denise was standing. She waved at Denise. She took the two children into the house. As the door closed, David hugged Denise.

"You should be very proud of this moment. You did a wonderful thing when you gave this house away long ago. How do you feel about this?"

"It is strange how I feel." She kept watching the children playing.

"I feel that there is closure in my heart now. It feels good to see this. There is a feeling that there is a conclusion and an ending to the war in my mind and my heart is full of happiness now I have seen this."

"You know what? I feel that too. Seeing you like this makes my war go away and if it weren't for you wanting to come here, I may never have felt it. Yes, my war is far away now."

"I love you David, so very much and you are right, the war has ended now. There are no bombs or fire and no more death."

They got back into the cab. She turned to David as they kissed.

"There is another place I would like to see very much David."

"And what and where is that?" She called to the cab driver.

"Take us to seven eighty and sixth street please."

They were holding hands as the cab driver stopped at the address.

"This is you address you wanted mam" David looked around and at her.

"Where are we?" She got out of the cab.

"Come, we walk." David got out and handed the driver a bill.

"Keep the rest for you."

"Merci beaucoup sir." He waved and drove off. They stood in the street.

"Look David, you can see the Embassy from here."

He looked down the street and looked at her smiling at him.

"You remember not this place?" She pointed to a building. David looked all around hoping to see something he recognized.

"That is our old apartment building, I think, but so much has changed."

"As you say, change is good no."

They stood in the middle of the street looking at the new buildings. She went to the address she wanted to see. She opened her purse and took something out. She walked to the front door step and put a tiny silver thimble down on the doorstep and went back to David. He stood looking at it. He took a step closer.

"That's a thimble, why did you do that?"

"This where we started David, I am hope it will bring them luck as it did with us. It brought us together and we can look at us now."

"Is that the same thimble I gave you in Paris on the pier?"

"No, I save the thimble you gave me in my jewelry box at home."

"Son of a gun, you are an amazing and wonderful woman."

She giggled. "If you say so, I think we have made a complete trip in our life. Don't you think so?"

"Yes, the circle has been completed now. I thought it would never have an ending but now, you made it happen by coming back here."

"David, there is one more place I would love to see again soon."

"And where might that be my sweet angel?"

"Home, I want to go to our home in America, can we go there?"

They started walking down the foggy Paris street holding hands.

"David, I ask you something okay?"

"Sure."

"You ever think of a family for us?"

"Ah, yes, a girl's soft ball team would be nice to have."

"Oh David, I love softball, can I play too?"

He laughed. "Anything you want lady, anything you want."

They and kissed and kissed. "I love you so very much."

And as you know, they were happy ever after,

The End

Hi, I want to thank you for reading, "Thimble" and I hope you have enjoyed reading it as much as I did in writing the book. I truly believe that Romance and Love is in all of our hearts and it will find us always.

For buying the book, I would like very much to give you a gift. I would like to send you free, two beautiful silver bracelets with a tiny silver "Thimble" attached. All you have to do to get this free gift from me is to write to me with your printed name, address, city, state, and zip code.

And address it to me at:
Robert Cory Phillips
8757 Old Charlotte Pike
Pegram, Tennessee 37143

Again, merci to you and tell a friend you have read "Thimble."

Robert Cory Phillips/Author

I would ask you for one thing. When you write for your gift please tell me:
Why did Denise and Charlotte go to the Mall, and what did they buy? Answer this question in your letter to me. Thank you very much.